THIS IS NOT AMERICA

THIS IS NOT AMERICA

STORIES

JORDI PUNTÍ

TRANSLATED FROM CATALAN
BY JULIE WARK

ATRIA BOOKS

New York London Toronto Sydney New Delhi

ATRIA
BOOKS

An Imprint of Simon & Schuster, Inc.
1230 Avenue of the Americas
New York, NY 10020

LLLL institut
ramon llull
Catalan Language and Culture

The translation of this work has been supported by the Institut Ramon Llull.

First Atria Books hardcover edition July 2019

ATRIA BOOKS and colophon are trademarks of Simon & Schuster, Inc.

For information about special discounts for bulk purchases, please contact Simon & Schuster Special Sales at 1-866-506-1949 or business@simonandschuster.com.

The Simon & Schuster Speakers Bureau can bring authors to your live event. For more information or to book an event contact the Simon & Schuster Speakers Bureau at 1-866-248-3049 or visit our website at www.simonspeakers.com.

Interior design by Suet Yee Chong

Manufactured in the United States of America

10 9 8 7 6 5 4 3 2 1

Library of Congress Cataloging-in-Publication Data has been applied for.

ISBN: 978-1-9821-0471-9
ISBN: 978-1-9821-0473-3 (ebook)

For Steffi

Contents

America is the neighbouring village,
any small village in Catalonia:
youngsters throw stones at gypsies,
people scowl at strangers,
the blacks are . . . are blacks,
the poor become rich there,
the young make their fortune
and in the fresh air beside the last few huts
there begins a heaven
                    which is open to everyone.

There you can be alone and with others,
you can roast green peppers and the aubergine,
crickets sing,
races mingle,
weeping is permitted there,
I can help you on with your socks,
we will gather, we will gather, we will gather
and the villages come together in their love.

Evenings in the bar strange individuals
come from nowhere, who don't know where they are,
lay down the law for the world now being invented,
Americans from Santander, from Barcelona
and the Catalans, Sioux and Mexicans
will own a new kind of petroleum
that has as yet no name nor will have ever
however often, shepherdess, you refuse
                    to serve me with the sacred gas.

America is the neighbouring village
in Granollers, Ametlla, Borges Blanques,
in Mataró, Morella, Cadaqués,
and in Montuïri eating chocolate.

ENRIC CASASSES, "AMÈRICA"
TRANSLATION BY ANNA CROWE

VERTICAL

He leaves the subway in Plaça d'en Joanic and, coming up the stairs into the night, hears some nearby church bells chiming ten. Maybe they're imaginary bells and they're only ringing in his head, but never mind. What counts is here and now. He repeats it mentally: here and now, right? He lights a cigarette and walks briskly down to Passeig de Sant Joan. There aren't many people in the street, not many cars, or it might just seem that way because the orangey glow from the streetlights is scattering arabesques of lackluster shadows everywhere. As he passes the churro shop in Carrer de l'Escorial, which is closed today, he shoos away a bittersweet memory. Not now, not yet. But then, just after that, at the top end of Passeig de Sant Joan, facing the half-hidden statue of a friar and a small boy, he stops for a few seconds and thinks of her. The thought is full of pain, yet hazy. A few days ago, and he can't be more specific than that, Mai's face started being wiped out of his memory . . . Well, not exactly that. He doesn't want to use a negative verb. Rather, it's been gently fading away, a vapory cloud of smoke, little by little, very slowly dispersing, and the days go by and you keep seeing it even though it's no longer there, and you reach a point when you can see it only because you can imagine it, because you've seen it before and you know it was there.

This sensation of impending oblivion is what's finally got him moving today. He looks up at the sky. It's a serene starry night. The warm air's playing with the leaves in the trees. Now resolved, he starts to walk, one step after the other. When he reaches the statue of Josep Anselm Clavé, he glances at it but doesn't stop. One day, years ago, they decided that this fusty, frock-coated fellow with his bushy moustache had to be someone more eminent than this Clavé. Someone really internationally famous. They started trying to work out who he looked like. Balzac. Nietzsche. Trotsky, but without the glasses. Wouldn't it be great if Barcelona had a statue of Trotsky? In the end, she came up with the best answer. Since he was holding a wand in his hand, it would be the statue of a famous magician from the days of the first illusionists and conjurers. Houdini, Max Malini . . . Clavini! The magician who, from his pedestal, made all the boring residents of Barcelona's Eixample neighborhood vanish into thin air!

The memory makes him smile for a moment—that wicked gleam in Mai's eye—but it immediately shrivels to leave a hollowness in his guts, so he walks faster trying to get rid of the nascent burning. He's got to get used to it, he tells himself, and this nighttime walk has to help him too. This might be why, when he gets to Carrer de la Indústria and stops at the traffic lights, he realizes he's been going too fast. He won't leave any trace if he rushes so much. The ink of his footsteps won't write anything. Then, like a man possessed, he turns around and runs back to the beginning of Passeig de Sant Joan, even overtaking two jogging boys. Sweating and panting with the effort, he stops and starts over, now more slowly.

—

Tonight he's walking to trace out the letter *I* in "Mai." Passeig de Sant Joan from end to end, right down to the Arc de Triomf. When they met up again, a million nights ago, he changed her name. She immediately agreed because she was convinced that every age deserves a different name, and she'd been waiting for this for quite a while. When she was a little girl her parents called her Maria Teresa. At school she became Teresa—Tere, to her closest friends and first boyfriend—and, a little later, at college, Maite. They'd seen each other around the Arts courtyard, and maybe they'd shared the odd conversation with mutual friends in the faculty bar. Then, all those years later, they met up again at a party in the Gràcia neighborhood, in an apartment that was too small, or too crowded with last-minute guests. A spring night, like now. Music of Echo & the Bunnymen, Ride, Pixies. They'd introduced themselves clinking beers and looking deep into each other's eyes. She moved her lips over the distortions of the guitars and he read there "Mai." A woman's name that could also mean Never. The day she moved her things into his place three weeks later, they fucked as if they had to celebrate the fact, and then she asked, "You're not one of those guys who gets tired of being with a woman . . . ?"

"No."

"I mean, you won't leave me or kick me out, will you?"

"Never, Mai. Never."

Then they fucked again and, still lying there all sweaty in the bed, cracked a bottle of Ballantine's and smoked some Afghan weed to keep the well-being going, or whatever it was they'd been wanting for such a long time. They were both thirty-four, a lousy age, and with more than one failure to forget about.

———

That was more than fifteen years ago, and right now he doesn't know if he's walking to forget it completely or to remember it all. Once again he's heading down Passeig de Sant Joan, more conscious of his steps, as if his shoes are leaving real prints in the asphalt, a sign that can be read from a bird's-eye view. He walks past the Great Clavini, and when he gets to the traffic lights at Carrer de Sant Antoni Maria Claret he notices the Bar Alaska there, on the left. It's full because there's a soccer match on TV. That's why there's no one out in the streets tonight. He wonders if he should go over for a moment, but there's no need. He can easily revive that family feeling: TV on, waiters in the typical getup, stinking of sweat, the permanent drunks . . . There was a time when he and Mai used to go out for beers with some friends who lived nearby. They called it the Chamfer Route. They'd meet on Saturdays, midafternoon, and started with beers in the Pirineus on the chamfered corner of Carrer de Bailèn. Then to the Alaska and the Sirena Verde, to end up in the Oller till they closed. In the Alaska, they always made fun of the other drinkers and laughed a lot. Old ladies who hung around there all afternoon badmouthing their kids over a pathetic Cacaolat; the separated guy at the bar getting into the cognac as he checked out dating ads; the couple who never spoke as they shared *patates braves* and a toasted ham-and-cheese sandwich for dinner (so they played at guessing who'd be beating up whom later that night). They stopped doing the Chamfer Route precisely because of soccer. The bars were packed with rowdy people and you couldn't talk or drink in peace.

He crosses at the lights. A bicycle goes past next to him and, heading down Passeig de Sant Joan, is soon lost in the gathering darkness. A young couple sitting on a bench is sharing a bag of chips. They eat one and kiss, another chip, another kiss. A dog goes over to them, a black schnauzer. The girl wants to give it a chip but the dog is old and lazy and can't decide. Then the owner whistles and the dog loses interest and turns tail. For a few seconds they're walking together, him and the dog, at the same pace. These instants make up a scene of workaday routine, and, more than anything, it bothers him. He and Mai never got used to that;

thinking about it a little more, it's clear to him they weren't into it at all. When the days started looking too much alike, when they achieved some semblance of normality—not that they made much effort—the thing always cracked at some weak point in the end. You would have thought that Mai's character was too unpredictable, too edgy, a lethal combination in itself, but there was more to it than that. Blame and risks were shared between the two of them, and that's probably why they loved each other with that unconditional madness. When they did love each other.

By the time he reaches Carrer de Còrsega, a sudden roar breaks into his thoughts. Someone's scored a goal. Fireworks are going off, like a dress rehearsal for Midsummer Eve. A driver festively toots his horn. He looks up and sees two boys who've come out onto a balcony to smoke. There are lights on in nearly every apartment. It's a warm night, and most windows are wide-open. Let the city noise come in now, when the heat's bearable, there are still no mosquitos, and Barcelona's streets don't stink of sewers. Suddenly that poem by Gil de Biedma comes to mind, the one called "Nights of the Month of June." They read it together and liked it a lot. It spoke of a night like this. He especially recalls the slightly melancholy mood, the student with his balcony doors open and, below, the recently washed street, the solitude, the uneasiness about all the unknowns of the future, but only a slight uneasiness . . . He tries to remember some of it and comes up with *a vaguely affective state of mind*, with that nicely placed adverb. But there was another more important line near the end . . . Now he can't get it.

The collection of poems by Gil de Biedma was the only book they had two copies of at home after they put their libraries together. They'd bought it when they were students, around the same time, and years later they reread it, looking for excuses for being the way they were, a poetic ploy to justify their actions. Here in the street, as he walks, it only takes a brief flashback to those hungover mornings of crusted vomit, the stale reek of cigarette smoke in the sheets, empty bottles and full ashtrays scattered on the floor—still life at the foot of the mattress—for the words he was looking for to pop into his head. *Pero también la vida nos sujeta porque precisamente no es como la esperábamos.* Yes, that's right. Life holds us fast, too, precisely because it is not as we thought it would be.

———

Mai's death left him stunned. It was a sense of unreality that at first numbed the hours and was like waking up comatose after you've been drinking nonstop for days, when you flow back disoriented and with a calm that inevitably runs off down some drain you never knew existed. He was sober but didn't seem it. They'd let him go back to work at the high school, and he did his classes on automatic pilot without thinking about what he was saying or getting pissed off with his students. He ate out, always locally and alone, sitting at the bar and never finishing what was on his plate. In that new, lonely netherworld Mai's absence overwhelmed everything, but it also held out periods of surprising lucidity. If he thought about her as if she were still alive,

7

he'd suddenly know what to do. And there was her betrayal with the whisky, if you can put it like that—eight months after they'd detoxed together yet again—but he forgave her more than anyone. He'd found her one Tuesday night when he came back from Prague after a school trip with his final-year students. She was lying on the sofa, naked, hair in a tangle, and her head hanging down in an unnatural position. She'd choked on her own vomit. Such a cliché death. If it hadn't been for her wide-open eyes and cold body, he would even have found her beautiful. It was a scene they'd already rehearsed together more than once, more than a couple of times.

The constant, stupefying confusion hasn't left him, but he's learned to live with it and sometimes he even tells himself he can manage it if she helps him. Like that day, quite a while after Mai was dead and cremated, when he decided that he had to write her name on the city. It was a game they'd played in the past, after the third detox which was theoretically the successful one. Once the jitters had calmed down and they were starting to be human again, the doctor recommended that they should walk every day, do some exercise, and, at the same time, chase away dangerous ideas. Then Mai remembered a book by Paul Auster in which his main character walks around the city, his steps tracing letters that are interpreted by someone coming behind him. They got a pencil and a map of Barcelona and began to imagine possible routes. They went out in midafternoon, when he got back from the school and she left her translations, and they walked or, more accurately, strolled around for an hour and a half. The grid layout of the Eixample neighborhood was ideal for monosyllables. Gràcia, Sants, and El Guinardó allowed calligraphic flourishes, while El Xino, a labyrinth of temptations, suggested garbled, dangerous graffiti, which was best to avoid.

———

Now, coming down Passeig de Sant Joan, he feels a sort of revival of the spirit of those walks, as if Mai were actually at his side. A few days ago, in an attack of longing, he started on the *M*, up Carrer de Muntaner, then continuing its strokes in the streets of Gràcia. The *A*, much more complicated to draw, was hidden in the ups and downs of the Putxet neighborhood. Now it pleased him that the *I* should be coming out from under his feet with this vertical simplicity, yet with the vigor of a nighttime downhill run. A single stroke and her name would be complete.

He's about to cross Carrer del Rosselló when he sees the famous journalist Joan de Sagarra going by, looking like he hasn't had dinner and gloomy and mad at the world or his neighborhood, or maybe mentally writing his next article in which he'll be mad at the world or his neighborhood. He knows that Sagarra lives around here because he's said so in more than one of his Sunday pieces. In a playground a little farther down, a small boy frenziedly climbs up and hurtles down a slide while a girl makes sure he doesn't hurt himself when he hits the bottom. He's about four or five and you can see he's hyper. His shouts echo in the absence of traffic. The girl, who must be his mother, is wearing a full-length turquoise sari with silver embroidery glittering under the streetlights. He watches her for a few seconds, guessing that she's not yet twenty-five and noting that she doesn't seem at all bothered that it's so late. Other children are at home sleeping, and this one has the whole playground to himself. He slows down, still looking with a touch of envy at the two figures, which seem to have been teleported from another faraway place at another time of day. A few meters farther along, he gets what's happening. On the other side of the street is a small Pakistani supermarket, and it's still open. From the doorway, a man is watching the movements of the mother and child. Get the kid tired and he'll drop off straightaway.

He keeps walking and now, yes, while he's lighting another cigarette, the memory he just had to suppress comes back. Late one night they went out for drinks and to dance in the Almo2bar, or whatever the dive was called, and they'd stopped to get churros in Carrer de l'Escorial. They'd eaten very little and drunk a lot, and, since they only smoked hash in those days, they were famished. They were eating the churros as they walked along, and Mai wanted to sit on one of the swings in the playground of Plaça d'en Joanic. He got behind her and, with a churro in his mouth, started pushing her. First he pushed gently, as if being careful with a small girl, but then, little by little, pushed harder and harder. Mai was laughing, screaming with extravagant fear, instinctively lifting and lowering her feet, but the swing, thrown out of kilter with her weight, was wobbling like crazy. In one of its lurches, just when she told him she'd had enough, her paper cone slipped out of her hand and two or three churros flew into the air. When she tried to grab them, she lost her balance. The fall, which left her flat on her back on the ground, was spectacular, clumsy, but harmless. He was laughing, and as he staggered over to help her up, the swing whacked his back and he also fell, next to Mai. The next day he'd have a bruise for sure, but now, trying to ignore the pain, he flung himself on top of her. They rolled around on the ground, locked together in a long kiss, a mix of laughter, churro dough, tobacco, and alcoholic spit.

"You see? We'd never be able to have kids, you and I," she blurted out in a pause, with a soberness that didn't match the happiness of the moment. "We wouldn't even know how to swing them, let alone parent them. Imagine what a disaster we'd be."

He was about to protest, but he knew Mai was right, so in response he hugged her tighter. Then, in the deeper voice that came out of him when he was tipsy and got all transcendental, he whispered, "*We'll* be our own kids."

They'd both turned forty.

———

They got fed up with everything. They'd been walking around, writing words in the streets of Barcelona for a while, when they decided they had to change things. Mai said it would be more fun if they followed each other, as in *The New York Trilogy*, and the one walking behind would decipher some kind of message along the way. Each of them had to imagine what the other was writing, but it wasn't easy, like when someone writes a word on your skin and your brain has to know what it is from the touch. Their conspiracy amused them. Sometimes, halfway through the walk, the pursuer caught up with the pursued, saying, "I'm lost. Start again." And they laughed at the absurdity, or guessed the end of the word and went to the writer to say "I love you too" (although they tried not to be too tacky). Since it was sometimes quite difficult to work out what was being written, he suggested that every time they finished a letter, they should pause to indicate a space by stopping and jumping, for example, or squatting to touch the ground. The plan lasted only a day, because the silly little jumps made Mai feel ridiculous. But one way or another they found new incentives to keep walking. They gave each other hints, like crossword clues.

"Today I'm going to write the name of a Russian novelist."

"Not 'Dostoyevsky,' eh. We'll never get to the end."

"Stop telling me what to do! Maybe I'll write 'Fyodor.'"

Sometimes the invisible word was related with the street they'd started out from, or they used the game to comment on everyday matters with monosyllabic shopping-list words—"juice," "bread," "milk"—but there were also days when they didn't feel like saying anything or were in a bad mood, and then they walked separately, wherever they wanted, randomly filling the city with unintelligible scribbles.

If someone had been watching them from the air, they would have looked crazy, or maybe as if they were acting out some sort of complicated sexual perversion. For them, however, it was just playing to keep boredom at bay in an alcohol-free evening or, more like it, fending off any tantalizing thoughts of booze, now they were on the wagon. They didn't talk about it much, but it seemed to them that their walks made the world go round, that their feet warmed the asphalt, as if they were helping to generate the energy that moves big cities. They didn't keep a record of the words they wrote and soon forgot them, but perhaps an imprint remained in the memory of the streets, as if all those invisible flourishes were ribbons and knots binding the two of them together, making them inseparable. So, in the times they weren't together, each was comforted by the idea that the other was walking round the city—at the other end of the thread—and they might link up at any moment.

He lights another cigarette and crosses Diagonal, hurrying because the traffic lights are about to turn red. Suddenly he has the sensation that someone's following him. He can almost hear footsteps. When he gets across the road, he turns, intent on seeing who it is. But he can't see anyone. It must be the specter of Mossèn Cinto, he tells himself, Verdaguer the poet-priest, stuck up there all alone on top of his column, struggling with the temptation to leap into the void. A few cars go by, tooting their horns and waving flags. So the match has ended well. Behind Mossèn Cinto, a bit farther on, as if hanging in the sky, the owl on top of the Roura building winks at him. With eyes like two phosphorescent yellow lanterns in the dark, the bird's a kind of superhero guarding over Barcelona's night people.

He'd decided to do this last walk at night because that was when Mai shone most. If it wasn't for his job teaching at the high school, which meant he often had to get up early, they would have ended up being denizens of the wee hours, urban vampires. Mai worked at her translations until late. She said that nightfall opened up the way for crossing between languages, and she'd only stop if he convinced her to go and see a movie in the late-night session at the Casablanca or the Arkadin. In winter they tended to stay at home, night creatures of inside realms. Sometimes, when she was still working, he'd go shopping, then boil up a saucepan of chicken and vegetables to make a three-day soup, which, when it was nearly finished, was warmed up again, padded out with a tot of whisky and a couple of egg yolks. At night they liked reading together, in their own worlds, or just chatting while they smoked some dope and listened to CDs. There was one by Pharoah Sanders that lasted exactly as long as the joints she rolled. Moreover, it was as if the music followed her mood swings. He'd eventually have to go to bed, but Mai stayed up. Sometimes she phoned a friend in Paris with the excuse of some problem with a translation, and, when they got talking about life, he was lulled to sleep by erotic murmurs in French coming from the next room.

At weekends or when the weather was nice and he wasn't teaching, any excuse was good enough for them to go out. They caught up with friends, went to concerts or to the Galician bar downstairs to have a beer, and if they were on some substance, they didn't get home till the next morning. They could never get enough of it, and it wasn't surprising that they took refuge in the night to avoid bad blood between them, as if it was neutral ground or constituted an armistice. For Mai, night wasn't a measure of time. It was a space, a thick, verdant forest that needed to be crossed from end to end, even if you didn't know what was waiting for you on the other side. And it was cheating to turn back. She said, "I don't care if we never come back from the night." He went along with that.

They were often out of control and got too squalid—well, a day is just a day, and each day was each day—but they looked after each other to the end. The next day they tended to wake up at home, in bed, in the middle of a devastated bedroomscape that seemed to have been attacked by machete blows, the result of some violence they didn't know about. Then the first one to wake up and see it blamed the other for the excess, and in the whole ritual they found some solace.

"Who am I doing this for?" he asks himself as he keeps walking down Passeig de Sant Joan. "Her or me?" The owl whispers in his ear, "For both of you, knucklehead." He heads down the wide pavement in a straight line and doesn't walk past anyone for a while. The bars are closing after the soccer fever and waiters are clearing the terraces with a racket of tables and chairs. He's walked more than half of the *I* and now he's afraid of finishing it. He slows down, stops for a moment, and feels ridiculous. Once again, he has the feeling that someone's coming up from behind, and even has a shiver of nearness but this time, too, there's no one there. Just the night. He lights up and starts walking again, trying to shake off the paranoia, convincing himself with every step that he's doing what he must do. No, he'll never forget her. Mai. Never. He knows that. If he's writing her name, it's only so the city will remember her.

———

When he gets to the Plaça de Tetuan, he hesitates for a few seconds, wondering whether to go round it to cross Gran Via or go straight through it. The iron gates of the park are still open and, though there's not much light inside, he goes in, because he has to keep the line of the *I* straight. In the shadows he can see three or four people talking in a ring, keeping an eye on their dogs, which are sniffing and chasing each other up and down the patches of grass. In the best-lit part, near the central group of sculptures, three adolescents are playing catch, trying to keep the ball in the air. They're shouting, yelling insults if one of them fumbles and drops it. A bit farther on, in the stripy shadows of palms and banana trees, he spots the silhouette of a couple lying on the ground but, walking past, realizes that, no, it's a hobo sleeping on a bed of cardboard and plastic bags. He keeps going and, just when he's about to leave from the far side of the square, he hears someone calling his name.

What surprises him most is that the voice sounds so calm and natural, as if it's been waiting for him. He stops and looks harder to see where it's coming from. Then he sees two figures coming toward him.

"It's you, right? What the hell are you doing here?" says

the voice. He immediately recognizes Toni Forajido, who vigorously pumps his hand as if they were pals having an arm-wrestling contest. He and Mai called him that because he played bass in a garage band named Los Forajidos. They had a couple of college friends in common and they'd seen them play at Sidecar or Magic, but he can't remember which. Then Toni left the band and went off to live in Berlin, after which they'd lost track of him.

"Nothing. Just walking, as you can see," he says, taking a couple of steps toward the gate of the park, where the glow from the streetlights is brighter. It's at least ten years since he's seen Toni, who's hollow-cheeked and hasn't aged well. It looks like he's still sporting the same old black leather jacket, cowboy boots, and earring that he wore back then, but over the years he's lost the air of outsider cockiness that bass players from all the bands around the world tend to have. "So, what are you two doing?"

"Gonna get wasted." Proud and solemn, Toni shows him two bottles of cheap vodka they must have bought five minutes ago. His roguish expression triggers the memory that Mai couldn't stand Toni Forajido, that she used to say that he was a poseur and a moron. "We worked hard today, so we earned it. Yeah, Christa?"

Then he notices the girl who's with Toni. She must be Polish or German, and if he put her age at eighteen, that would be pushing it. Her upper lip is pierced, so her smile looks mocking, and her blond hair is a snarled mess. It must be days since she's washed it. When he says hello, she looks at him with ill-concealed impatience. She seems tired, as if she'd rather sleep than get drunk. Toni Forajido strokes her back, tenderly caresses her cheek, and, with a wink at his old friend, asks if he'd like to join in the fun.

"No, thanks," he says. "I'll pass."

"You still see anyone from the old days?" Toni asks. "We were such a bunch of animals."

He shakes his head, saying no as neutrally as he can because he doesn't want to get into a conversation, let alone rake over old coals. He wants to go, leave them to it, and meanwhile the girl's starting to walk backwards, shuffling away to let them know it's about time he did go. Before saying goodbye, Toni Forajido asks, "By the way, are you still with that woman? Mai, right? She was a bit . . . well, I don't know how to put it, but, jeez, she had a spectacular ass and she liked a good time. Yeah, I remember her well."

"Right, right, we've been together for years." He doesn't want to tell the truth. Mai would see it as a defeat, and there's no need. Then they say goodbye and go their separate ways, but at the last minute he stops and shouts, "Hey, Toni, just a matter of curiosity: Do you still play bass?"

Toni Forajido doesn't say a word but raises his open left hand, waggling it as if waving. In that light he's just got time to notice that there's a finger missing, the middle one.

———

He's now on the last stretch of Passeig de Sant Joan and his feet are heavy. He's done. The ink's getting thicker. He thinks about the fluke of coming across Toni Forajido, today of all days, imagining the scrapes that have turned him into this seedy loser, a dopehead who picks up girls at railway stations or youth hostels or whatever. He also thinks about the way he referred to Mai. At first he felt flattered that Toni Forajido still remembered her after all those years, but was riled, too, by the offhand way he spoke about her. Now he feels bad for not objecting. They've known each other since the worst days (or best, depending on how you look at it) and he suddenly gets a mean idea: Toni, that bum, could have died and not Mai. Like a prisoner swap, except, in the end, it wouldn't have been any use either.

Now he can see the Arc de Triomf. There are more people going up and down in this section of the street, maybe because the subway's nearby. A couple gets out of a taxi and goes into a building. He watches them, can see them entering, waiting for the elevator, how he loosens his tie and she laughs at something. When he crosses Ausiàs March, he once again has the feeling that someone's coming behind him. He stops and a peppy girl with long, dark hair, jeans, blue sneakers, and a "spectacular ass" strides past, and he can't help shouting, "Hey!" His voice comes out fretful, almost desperate. The girl hesitates for a moment or two but doesn't turn around. On the contrary, she walks even faster and he knows he can't follow her.

As if needing some sign, he stops a few meters farther on in front of Norma Comics. Mai came here often. She loved comics. Through her, in their early days, he discovered *Métal Hurlant*, the brutal style of *RanXerox*, and Tardi's war stories. They lost themselves in Moebius's dreamworlds, and got worked up over Guido Crepax's Valentina. He checks out the comics in the window, the names of superheroes he doesn't know, the rubber figures of Tintin and Snowy, a life-size poster of one of Milo Manara's beauties. He examines it all with an intensity that's rare for this hour of the night. If it were open he'd go in. You might think he's dragging out the time before coming to the end. But it's not really that. He has a craving that can't be satisfied.

After a while, he starts walking again. At what point does writing a letter end if you can't lift the ballpoint from the paper? He walks under the Arc de Triomf and then realizes that Mai's name is now written on the city. He stops. He wants to cry but manages not to. He wipes his nose on his sleeve and lights up again. All at once, it's as if she's there, standing in front of him, more alive than ever, a fleeting presence with long, translucent hair, a weightless hand tugging at the other end of the narrative thread, pulling it tight. He looks at his sneakers. If he keeps walking now, the line won't end. There are no rules today. This isn't a game. He takes them off and keeps walking, barefoot, with the shoes in his hand. For a few seconds he's not sure where to go, but Mai shows the way—go right—and he enters the cramped space of Carrer del Rec Comtal, heading for the narrow streets of La Ribera, looking for the darkest alleys. He pats his back pocket, where he always carries his wallet. Luckily he remembered to grab some cash before leaving home.

BLINKER

I'm the briefcase guy and I hitch rides. Everyone knows me. Well, when I say "everyone," I mean all the folk who regularly take the road from Vic to Sant Quirze, or from Sant Quirze to Vic and beyond. Hundreds of people who, one day or another, have glanced at me when they've driven past, or looked at me with a sneer as if they're bothered by the fact that I'm there all alone, or deliberately avoided eye contact. Sometimes I imagine them at home, having dinner, looking for something to talk about.

"Today I saw that guy hitching just outside Vic. The briefcase guy."

"That's creepy," she says with a pointless shiver that starts and stops right there.

They say these things because I've got a clown's face—a clown without makeup—and everyone knows that clowns are scary, especially out of context and with no kids to amuse. I know because I look in the mirror at home and pull faces. I can see that I've got an agreeable, confident expression, but it only takes the movement of a couple of muscles to contract it into a grim mask. My reddened, slightly bulbous nose (rosacea, not booze), big mouth, thick, arched eyebrows, round head, and curly hair all conspire to turn me into a diabolical goblin or, worse, a diabolical old man on the lookout for heaven knows what. So I try not to laugh much. That, and because I'm getting old.

Part of the problem, well, if it must be called a problem and not prejudice, is the briefcase, which is black and of a normal size. A traveling salesman's briefcase. I've discovered that if I hitch with the bag on the ground beside me, they stop more than when I'm thumbing a ride with my right hand and hanging on to the handle with the left one. It must be because then it looks as if I'm on the move, in a hurry to get someplace, or maybe fleeing from some thorny situation, and normally people don't go looking for problems.

You keep discovering these kinds of details over time. At first, when it started to get cold in those milky-misted mornings of fall, I used to wear a long coat with a tartan flannel lining, which I'd inherited from a traveling-salesman uncle. It didn't take me long to work out that it did me no favors. There were drivers who beeped at me with a cynical grin or who, crawling past, opened the window to say "Fag" or "Perv." People are influenced by clichés they see on television, and a guy standing on the road with his coat half buttoned has to be a flasher. Then I got myself a black priest-style coat and it was plain sailing after that. The tie, too, you understand? That didn't fit with the image of a hitchhiker. A man wearing a tie must have a car, and, if not, he's faking and there's something fishy about him. Swindler, pusher, gangster . . . Once the cops even stopped and asked to see my ID.

I'm telling you all this from my own experience. I've been hitching four times a week for more than fifteen years, always Tuesdays and Fridays (except in vacation periods and national holidays, when I move my schedule one day forward), always the same route, and always the same time frames, too: midmorning and midafternoon. Fifteen years is a long time: many miles, many faces, many cars, and many conversations with strangers. I've got into all kinds of vehicles, even vans and trucks, and once I was picked up by a Porsche 911 driven by a kid who chewed gum nonstop. I've seen how car interiors change. Good upholstery replacing pleather or faux leather, or whatever they call it, tape decks getting more sophisticated, and smokers who put their faith in those vile-smelling air fresheners cut to look like a fir tree. I've seen how the roads around Vic have changed, with more and more traffic circles, and how, by the roadsides, fields and pastureland have been filling up with industrial buildings.

People's attitudes have changed, too. That's inevitable, but from the standpoint of hitching they've got worse if anything. Women driving alone never pick me up now—never—and when they're with a guy, they'll make him renege at the last minute for sure—that's if he ever intended to stop. (If I had to count the times, during all these years, that I've been picked up by a woman driving alone, I doubt I'd get to more than twenty, and I must say each time was worthy of celebration, as I'll explain later.) Maybe young people are more open and know better what they want than before, but I still try to avoid them, because they drive like bolting horses, and anyway, conversation isn't their thing. They're hotheads. Wet behind the ears. Over the years I've become a bit of a sybarite, if I can put it like that, and I have to be really desperate to get in a car with two or three kids. They stop, open the window, and out comes loud music and gusts of sweet smoke. Sure, these are signs.

So here you have one of the paradoxes of hitchhiking. I'm scared of some drivers and they're scared of me. Yet, actually, it's simple. You flick your blinker on, stop for a few seconds, lower your window, look the hitchhiker in the eye, ask where he's going, and say, "OK, get in." And if you don't trust him, you lie. "Sorry, I'm going somewhere else." That works for them and for me. I know there's one thing that complicates everything, of course: the damn briefcase. The mystery of the briefcase. What's inside it. Since a driver only has a few seconds to decide, the imagination has to work very fast. There are "before" people and "after" people. Some see the hatchet I'm going to use to kill them and chop them up. Others, bundles of banknotes I've stolen from someone I've already killed. Some ask me as soon as I get in the car, to break the ice and maybe to drive away dark forebodings: "So, are you a traveling salesman?" They think they know me, or they've seen me somewhere, or they feel sort of superior because they're helping me.

Sometimes I can see they're tense, so I prefer to lie, because that calms them. I say, "Yeah, that's right." I have several answers, perfected by habit or my TV-schooled imagination. "So, are you a traveling salesman?" they ask.

"At least I try," I say, patting the briefcase.

"You got me! Guilty!" I raise my hand as if about to swear on the Bible.

"Yes, but don't worry, I won't try to sell you anything," I say.

It's not always easy, but I try to guide the conversation so they don't go changing the subject and come up with something weird. I invent a kind of salesman's job, but it has to be something big so I can't carry samples, only catalogues, which I won't get out because I don't want to bore them. I represent a company making construction cranes. I sell garden swimming pools. I specialize in cinema seats. I've invented a lot of professions for myself, and more than once I've had to improvise an expert's description, piling on unnecessary details and absurd technical flourishes, which are more difficult to detect.

I must admit that at moments like this the adrenaline of deceit makes me sweat, yet it also gives me a feeling of inner well-being, as if at last what I've been doing all these years is really paying off.

Then, by way of counterpoint, I also want to note that some drivers don't open their mouths in the twenty-some minutes of the ride. They're not bothered by silence and don't turn on the radio or anything. You sit beside them and it's as if you're not there. They've done enough by inviting you to get in. If you try to start up a conversation out of courtesy, they answer with a single word, which might be timid like a lamb bleating or threatening like a lion's roar. You immediately understand that it's best to leave them alone. Then, since you know every inch of the landscape, you discreetly check out the inside of the car and put together a portrait of the driver using the signs you pick up: if he's one of those people who wash the car every Sunday because they don't know what to do with their free time; if he's nervous because he's grabbing the steering wheel too tight; if he's slack because the cancer awareness ribbon hanging off his rearview mirror is from five years ago. You have to do it, have to find some moments of mental escape, because if you don't, there comes a point when the silence solidifies in the car and starts stabbing at your temples and thumping in your chest, you sink lower and lower in the seat, the seat belt starts throttling you, and the road threatens to swallow you in its darkness. You feel dizzy and close your eyes, and you know he won't turn to look at you because, for him, you're not there. Sometimes this bad scene lasts only a few seconds, but other times you get out of the car numb and downhearted, with the sensation that the trip has lasted three long, long years, during which you've rapidly aged. All your muscles ache, and you stretch your legs as if you've just crossed half Europe in one go. Yes, there are days like that.

———

One of the usual questions they ask when I get in a car is why I hitch rides at my age. Some mention the age thing with a touch of disdain or concern, as if they think I'm addled or something, because they consider it's unlikely that I'd be doing it because I want to. Others take it for granted that it's just this once—that I'm in a tight spot and forced to do it. So they're astonished when I tell them I don't have a car or a driver's license and this is how I get around when I'm doing my job.

What I don't tell them is that I started almost by accident. I like my sleep and the first day I had to go to Vic with my brand-new briefcase, I missed the bus. The next bus was an hour later and I was left standing there, instinctively thumbing a ride, like I'd seen the young folks doing. I didn't even have to wait five minutes before someone picked me up. By the time we got to the straight stretch near Sant Hipòlit, we'd already overtaken the bus. There are habits that start out of carelessness or pressing need, and you don't imagine they'll eventually become a lasting routine. One day you hitch a ride. Another day you wear suspenders instead of a belt. Or you invent a sister who lives in London, for example, a yoga teacher, for example, Lady Di's personal trainer, for example, and they all fall for it because it's easier and nicer to believe it than not believe it, and, after all, they can always use it to brighten up an after-dinner conversation with their friends.

"The other day I picked up this guy who was hitching a ride on the outskirts of Vic and he told me an amazing story . . ."

I must say, too, that in all these years, I've never been picked up by anyone famous. Friends, acquaintances, people I know by sight, yes, but the ones you see on TV or in the newspapers, no. The Barcelona taxi drivers like to recall the day they picked up the crooner, the politician, the stand-up comedian (who always grandstands, a disagreeable guy). It doesn't work in reverse. The art of hitchhiking only lets you meet normal, ordinary folk. Or so they seem. You open the door, get superficially involved in their lives for a while, then you get out of the car, and they forget you and you forget them. That's the theory, anyway, because reality changes the plan and puts you to the test. For instance, I wouldn't wish it on anyone to have that feeling that you've just gotten into a stolen car. You realize a second too late, when you're already in it with your seat belt fastened. He starts driving and he's ham-fisted because he doesn't know the car. It's only guessing, of course, and he doesn't tell you, but it's happened to me two or three times. You feel trapped, you know you can't escape, and you'd better just keep still and quiet till you get to the end of the ride. Then you go past a patrol car—stopped at a traffic light, or lying in wait in a side road—and, just before that, the stranger slows down and asks you some stock question, starts chatting, and then you understand you're playing a role. You have to. You're someone who's creating a harmonious atmosphere, someone who's cheating the math of the suspect all alone in the stolen car. Your anonymous, serene face is the dad's, the brother-in-law's, the colleague's, the best buddy's. You give a dose of normality to the scene, and he could be a terrorist, a kidnapper, or some punk thief (and God knows what's in the trunk, you think in a moment of lucidity), and you make an effort to play the unwritten part you've been scripted, smiling and responding as best you can. Then, as soon as the cops are out of sight, the dense silence is back and you, relieved, are clutching your briefcase and watching the road. When you finally come into your town and he asks where you want to stop, you say anywhere's fine, mainly so he won't find out where you live and how you earn your living. Just in case someone turns him in and then he comes looking for you.

So, as you see, thumbing a ride is chancing it because it leaves you at the mercy of others. Sometimes you have to amuse yourself by counting cars. The eighth one will stop, you tell yourself, convinced, and it stops. The next red car will stop, you tell yourself in despair, and it doesn't. You have to imagine a lot of ways of passing the time if you want to stay in a good mood.

I already mentioned the days when more women drivers picked me up than now. I really liked that! Such determination to fill silences. Such relaxing rides. I wished they'd never end. Things to talk about came up effortlessly and rarely slipped into clichés—soccer or work. I never had to hide a yawn in the presence of a woman driver. And, as I also said before, I have a special face, but I'm still convinced that some women knew how to read in it the goodness of a confidant. There were some who, as soon as I got in the car, took the conversation into matters that interested them most just then, as if my mission was to bring out a train of thought, act as a mirror, or be their handball wall. I listened to grumbles about baselessly jealous husbands, consoled a girl who knew her guy was cheating on her and encouraged her to act, and tried to open the eyes and soul of a woman from my town who was about to marry a total imbecile. I don't feel at all bad about acknowledging that I even made the day of a widow from Ripoll who must be twenty years older than me and was looking for I don't know what, but maybe some wild adventure to shake her out of her monotony in the most novelettish way. A week later we did it again in the same roadside hideaway, but we both realized it was a one-day wonder. When she let me out in Sant Quirze, she patted my cheek with a maternal gesture and thanked me with shining eyes: she was almost lost forever, but I got her back on track with just one shake-up (her words).

I know that this account of female rides sounds over-the-top. It must be nostalgia. Then again, I suffered once, too. Years ago, one Tuesday afternoon in Vic, I was picked up by a woman who could have changed my life but she didn't. You know when all of a sudden you're sure you've found your other half? Ten minutes, there in the car, were enough for me to see we were made for each other. Of course, it was a too-premature conclusion—the stuff of frustrated loves, as we know—but it was the first time I was in no doubt. I've half forgotten what we talked about—probably nothing important, though for a while afterwards I relived every second at her side, every nuance of every inflection of her voice, trying to extract useless hopes. It was raining—that I do remember—and as soon as I got in, she said she'd stopped because she felt sorry for me.

The Seattle Public Library
Southwest Branch
Visit us on the Web: www.spl.org

Checked Out Items 10/1/2019 19:19
XXXXXXXXX7303

Item Title	Due Date
0010084007292	10/22/2019
Like water for chocolate : a novel in monthly installments, with recipes, romances, and home remedies	
0010096202519	10/22/2019
Field of bones	
010099412578	10/22/2019
This is not America : stories	
010099468232	10/15/2019
We are Puget Sound : discovering and recovering the Salish Sea	

# of Items: 4

Renewals: 206-386-4190
TeleCirc: 206-386-9015 / 24 hours a day
Online: myaccount.spl.org

South Park Branch reopens
June 10 at 1 p.m.

"You looked like a wet dog out there . . ." Her tone was lighthearted. She almost seemed to be making fun of me, but there was also a hint of tenderness I'd never experienced before.

"Woof, woof," I said, playing along. Touching my wet ringlets, I asked, "Can I shake off the water in here?"

"Heaven help you if you do!" she said, laughing.

Then we got into a conversation that would have been boring for anyone else. I'm not the sort of guy who wants to set the world to rights with everything I say, and I don't think she's like that either. I remember one thing she said, and very naturally: the strap of a new bra was cutting into her flesh and she couldn't wait to get home to take it off. She also asked me about the briefcase. I told her the truth and she made an amused comment, something I'd actually thought myself some time before. We laughed about it together and our laughter sounded very good. We were making music. But the important thing wasn't what but how, the sensation that it all came from an earlier intimacy, as if someone had prepared us in a previous life, or as if that familiarity wasn't totally new but written in our genes.

What is it that bugs me most about the whole thing? Well, I'm not sure whether it was the same for her, even though for some months I was convinced it was.

At the time, I was living alone. I was burning inside with the need to find someone. By my town's standards I was getting old. Bachelor status was hovering over me. On Saturday nights I went out for beers with two friends, and we played pool at the bar. Then we did the rounds of the local discos till daybreak, but we almost always ended up having a croissant fresh from the oven at the Pavicsa bakery and going home alone. The afternoon I met that woman—I never found out her name but only noted the model and color of her car, a white Renault 5, when she was driving away down the road—all that investment in time and alcohol became pitiful, ridiculous. My excitement was so pure, it didn't cross my mind that I'd never see her again. On the contrary, the following Tuesday, impelled by a kind of amorous superstition, I repeated the same movements at the same time, but she didn't go past. *OK, so she only does the route on Fridays,* I told myself with the security of a man deciphering an easy riddle, so I repeated the same ritual on the Friday. I almost wished it would rain as it had done the previous week and, if possible, with the same drops and everything, but my lady, my stranger, didn't come along. She never came along afterwards either. Even now, when I see a white Renault 5 approaching, my heart leaps.

In all these years of hitchhiking, as is logical, there have been short and long waits. There are days when you just have to stick up your thumb and days when you're at it for so long that your arm starts cramping. In the end you work out the average, and one wait makes up for another, but I remember getting quite desperate on three or four occasions. Of course, the worst time was after my brief encounter with the love of my life. The following Friday, since she didn't come along at the same time as the previous week, I decided to wait for her. I stood back a little, a couple of steps, so the drivers could see me but wouldn't stop. A young guy, a student, also hitchhiking, joined me, and I was terrified she'd take him and not me (then I might have done something stupid) but luckily someone soon picked him up. Bye-bye. Meanwhile I was there, patiently waiting, convinced she'd see me and stop. I'd invite her to a beer and speak clearly. An hour slipped by, two hours slipped by, three, but I didn't lose hope. A couple of cars I know stopped, people from my town inviting me to get in, but it wasn't her, so I made up some excuse. It got dark. The lights in the houses came on and then it was dinnertime. I morphed into a sinister shadow in the tawny glow of the streetlights. I'm sure you can imagine it. Those times when nobody picks you up and you're left out in the cold are horrible. You brood for brooding's sake, to pass the time, and you come to the conclusion you're all alone in the world, the last survivor, a road Robinson Crusoe, until you're dazzled by the headlights of an approaching car, which accelerates to forget you all the faster. Then you're jolted back into the real world.

At around eleven the cars started to go by more regularly, people with full bellies coming home from dinners, crazy groups out for a wild time on a Friday night. I would have been a nuisance for them, and the real traveling salesmen who were coming home after spending all day in Barcelona were too tired. In the dark, the briefcase was blacker and more threatening. Around midnight I gave up. I was a nobody, I was shattered, and for the first and only time in my life I didn't get into any car and spent the night in Vic. Not far away, there was a pension on the Ronda Camprodon, and as I'd envisioned in anxious moments on other difficult evenings, I slunk over there that night and took a simple room like a monk's cell. The bed, nightstand, and overlarge TV without remote control came together in a perfect setting for mortifying myself by thinking about the woman of my life. I remember almost nothing of that night in purgatory, which went by in dreams and obsessions, but I do recall that at one point I woke up, opened the drawer in the nightstand, and discovered a Bible. I was so off my head that if I'd found a loaded pistol in there, I would have shot myself on the spot.

I'm carrying on about these fixes you get into when you're hitchhiking, but I don't want to seem sneering or ungrateful. It must be said that drivers are almost always friendly and open, and before long you get into a conversation about public affairs in the region. That some or other mayor has been seen going to a whorehouse. That some farmers do what they damn well like with their liquid manure. If that restaurant in Vic has closed, well, you could see it coming. There was one—a guy called Manubens from Campdevànol—who, for almost a year, picked me up every Tuesday on the way home. After four or five times I didn't even have to stick up my thumb. Since he always went by at the same hour, I waited in the same place, outside a stationer's that turned into a computer shop years later, and he'd pick me up in a Ford Fiesta, I think it was. We got on well. He was older than me and at first he was a bit cagey, but we got friendlier and friendlier with each ride. We remembered each other's opinions, we knew how to listen, and we watched our words to avoid any areas of conflict. I remember that it was at the end of the nineties because he couldn't stand all the bullshit about the millennium effect. He said it was just tricks of the Americans to make idiots of us and keep us under control, and for similar reasons he also ranted about cell phones. He swore he'd never have one because they turn you into a slave. (I'd like to see him now.) Another thing that got him wound up, but he kept going on about it, was killing time when you're on sick leave and you have to stay home, fighting about everything with your wife. Manubens always wore a tracksuit, a dark green, slightly old-fashioned model, vaguely military, vaguely Brazilian, with yellow stripes down the sides. You could see he wasn't used to it and that, deep down, he felt ridiculous, but it was a question of comfort. The second ride he told me he was doing rehab at the hospital. He was a bricklayer, and some time back he'd had a serious accident, something to do with scaffolding, though you couldn't see any outward sign of what happened. When I asked him about it, he brushed it off with a few vague comments. It was clear he didn't want to talk about it, yet he did have a tic that gave him away. He'd quickly touch the back of his neck as if tracing the line of a scar under his thinning hair. Another day it escaped him that the matter was with the lawyers and that someone had died, a poor kid who hadn't even seen it coming. Yeah, so you fall badly and you're done for. Then his mouth twisted in a grimace of pain as if he was being tortured for talking too much, so I didn't ask him about it anymore.

One afternoon, about ten months after we started meeting up every Tuesday, the car broke down just after the bend near the Can Pantano restaurant. There was a sudden cracking sound, followed by a screech. Manubens immediately braked and pulled over. I thought it was a flat.

"Shit!" he said, and we both got out of the car. Watching him walking, I noticed he had a limp, as if one of his legs, I don't remember which, wasn't strong and dragged a little. He was taller and ganglier than he seemed when he was behind the wheel, and in the daylight he appeared older, too. He opened the hood, looked inside, and made an instant diagnosis. "It's the fan belt. Just as I thought. Lucky we stopped straightaway."

So it's the fan belt. Sure it is, I thought, but I don't know about these things. He had a spare in the trunk and set about changing it. Out of courtesy I offered to help, but with his head buried in the engine he said no need. He'd be done in ten minutes. Since I was getting in the way, I went to stretch my legs by the roadside. It was getting dark, a time when not many cars were going past. I think it must have been April, as the barley fields were rippling in different tones of green depending on whether, at that hour, the sun shone on them or not. A few meters farther on, at the end of the bend, I noticed there was some guardrail and someone had tied a bunch of red roses on it. I touched them. They'd withered but weren't totally dry. There must have been a fatal accident not long before, or maybe it was the anniversary of a fatal accident. Then, looking for signs, my gaze went to the bank rising by the roadside. Although there was no broken glass or oil stains or anything else on the asphalt—someone had carefully cleaned it up—the earth and weeds were dug up or flattened in some places, so it wasn't difficult to imagine the metal tangle of the car that had smashed through the rail, the violent crash, the sliding back down. (That's why I never got a driver's license.) Just when I turned around to go back to the car, something on the ground caught my eye: a cassette tape without its box, lying there in the grass. I picked it up. It was a BASF and someone had written on both sides *Party, Party, Party.*

A shout from Manubens, who'd finished changing the fan belt, broke into my train of thought. As I was on my way back to the car, he started the engine, and for a moment I thought he was going to leave me there and drive off with my briefcase. That was stupid, but maybe it was because of this strange fear, or to explain why I'd made him wait, or to distract us from the scare, I showed him the cassette.

"Look what I found on the ground over there," I said, once inside the car. I didn't mention the bunch of flowers.

"Do you think it will work? Go on. Try it."

"I think it's OK," I said. "If you like it, you can keep it."

Now that I know what happened afterwards, it all seems like a bad joke.

He opened the tape deck, took out the tape from inside it, slipped in the new one, and pressed PLAY. There were a few seconds of silence, and just when we were about to forget about listening to it, a deep voice came out of the speakers, slowly getting higher—the tape was stretching—until we could hear some cheerful music. Manubens smiled. It was a song I'd heard dozens of times, by an English band of my day. Supertramp, maybe? I wasn't sure, but suddenly I thought that this was the song the person who'd had the accident was listening to, and was overcome with a hypocritical feeling of anguish, as if we had no right to be doing this, as if we were profaning the last few seconds of another person's life. Manubens didn't notice, and as soon as the next song began he said, "Yeah, I know this one! That's ABBA, right? They won the Eurovision contest years ago."

I nodded. The dark had swallowed up the last rays of sunlight and we were approaching Orís. Then, halfway through the song, which was "Waterloo," the music sped up. The singers started to sound off-key and there was a grotesque howling, as if the tape had slackened or knotted inside the deck. Anyway, it was like someone was pitilessly torturing them. In a couple of seconds the music turned mournful, like the way I imagine psychophony would sound. Then it sounded like wailing from beyond the grave mingled with baby cries. The effect was comical and I burst out laughing, but somewhat hysterically. And suddenly Manubens pulled over to the roadside, braked sharply, almost skidding, and indignantly turned off the music, pulled the tape out, opened the window, and threw it away, into the dark again. The tape had broken inside the deck, was frayed, and it flew off with a varnishy snap.

"Where did you get that thing?" he shouted. "Who are you? What harm are you trying to do to me?"

"Me? Nothing . . . ," I mumbled, innocent and shocked by his reaction. I don't know if he heard me. In the shadows I could only see his contorted face. It was as if those brutal, savage sounds had taken him back to a place or time that absolutely terrified him. Maybe it was related with his mishap at work, but I don't know. Maybe he'd put two and two together and in those shrieks he'd heard echoes of the voices of the accident a few miles back. The pain of others is a mystery that binds us, and it's too much for us at times, so we don't know how to react. I was so astonished, I didn't dare to say anything else. He didn't say anything else either. He started driving again and five minutes later, we reached Sant Quirze. He left me at the usual place and I thanked him when I got out. His only response was a nod. *Go on, off you go.* He was glad to get me out of his sight.

———

In my years of hitchhiking I've seen everything, but I think this story, the Manubens one, sums up well the strangeness of all people without exception, this thing we usually call inner life, which is manifested in a thousand unforeseen and contradictory ways. The following Tuesday, at the usual time, I waited in the same spot as every other week. I believed that Manubens would pick me up and we could talk about it. I'd even rehearsed some kind of apology, but there was no sign of him. Maybe he'd finished his rehab, or so I made myself believe. All in all, a road has great evocative power, and every time I pass that spot, just after the Can Pantano bend, I relive a few seconds of that April evening with Manubens. Sometimes I look at the bunch of flowers tied to the guardrail, with drier roses or, once again, fresher ones, reading them as a warning to be careful. Sometimes I think about those hellish screeches coming out of the tape deck and memory makes too much of them. Then the odometer keeps ticking over and I forget it all again, of course.

I think I already said that I have this tendency to make up stories, which is a reaction to the forced socializing, a defense mechanism if you like. It's been many years, and I'm tempted by an abstract image: me breaking down into little bits in every one of the cars that's picked me up, inhabiting them eternally until the day comes when they drive over a precipice, or quietly gather dust in a village garage, or docilely head for a car cemetery, where they'll rust in the rain and under the sun till a machine crushes them into a block of steel.

Countering these mental wanderings, there are days when I also think that my legacy of all those years on the road is that I've turned into an urban legend. Or rural. Depends how you look at it. A variation on the famous theme of the girl who was hitchhiking one dark night and disappeared on the same bend where someone had died in an accident years earlier. Except that I haven't died. There are drivers who've been seeing me for years, who know who I am, and yet they still drive past. One day I won't be there and they'll still keep seeing me. That'll be my little bit of posterity.

KIDNEY

The first letter arrived at midday one Tuesday, but Gori didn't open it until almost a week later. He didn't open it because he didn't feel like it. Now that he'd left his health problems behind, his life was trundling on without any dramas. Anyway, for some absurd reason that he'd forgotten, he always opened his mail on Monday nights. So the very few letters he received piled up on a wicker chair by the door together with bank receipts, advertising leaflets, and the College of Pediatricians journal, which arrived punctually every two months in the name of the former tenant.

Gori, then, dealt with the mail the following Monday night, sitting at the kitchen table and waiting for the spaghetti to cook. He opened the letters with a knife, glanced at them, and decided which ones he needed to keep and which he didn't. When he picked up the envelope that started this whole story, he immediately recognized his brother's hand. There was no sender, but looking at his own name and address was enough. The writing was lean, with vigorous strokes, bony looking. The capital *T* was like a tibia and the *c*'s were both rounded and angular, like the cheekbone of a Russian model. Studying the letters, he remembered an article he'd once read in a Sunday magazine. A serious graphologist explained that we acquire the basic script we'll have for the rest of our lives at about the age of twelve, after which the writing evolves with us as we become adults. Only people who are very sure of themselves or very superstitious always keep the same style without perceptible variations.

Reluctantly, as if he didn't quite believe it, he opened the envelope, took out the piece of paper that was folded in half, and read it. His brother's same old insolent writing. It was undated, unsigned. There was just one sentence.

I'll be needing a kidney.

Gori instantly understood what his brother was asking of him but didn't react in any way, either well or badly. He folded the sheet of paper again to put it back in the envelope and then saw that there was something else inside. He took it out. It was a check for three thousand euros, made out to the bearer. Yeah, right. He suppressed a scornful smirk with a sigh of pity. Then he tore up the envelope, letter, and check and threw the scraps in the trash can. The spaghetti would be ready. He was hungry. He hadn't seen his brother for thirty years.

———

Gori had suffered attacks of loneliness throughout his adult-hood. They were infrequent, mostly benign, but they came without warning and swamped him all day long with false nostalgia for the past, springing not from memory but imagi-nation. He fretfully wondered where life would have taken him if he hadn't walked out the way he did three decades ago. The answers were always flights of fancy and, like teen-age comedy movies, had the virtue of soothing his low spirits.

Now he lived alone. Had done for the last four years. Or was it five? He'd lost count. He'd had long periods with a lot of amorous activity, when one girlfriend replaced another without leaving enough time for him to feel aban-doned, and then he'd even lived nine years, three months, and eighteen days with the same woman. He had a few friends, too. In the beginning he forced himself to social-ize. *In a village you've got to have some proper friends or you'll rot away,* he told himself. He often went down to the café at night to play dominos, Sunday mornings he rode his bike on the mountain tracks, and he visited the library and took out books people recommended to him.

Sometimes, in these attacks of loneliness when he felt that the house was closing in on him—as if all the laugh-ter and conversations of a happy past had been eating away at the wooden beams—Gori brooded over what his death would be like. He wondered who'd find him, if he'd suf-fer a lot, what would happen to his things; but they were more like rhetorical questions, and they helped him to feel sorry for himself. He'd been through a hard time with his health, but his friends had made sure he was never alone.

Moreover, he hadn't taken anything with him from home. Thirty years ago he'd left without saying goodbye. He'd just turned eighteen then. He was the younger son, but his brother was only fourteen months older. People said they looked like twins. He found it hard to understand how, after coming out of the same belly and pumping the same blood, life had made them so different.

Gori had left without warning, in a fit of rebellion and rage. Time had helped him to understand that it hadn't been a hasty, crazy decision but something that had been ripening for ages, perhaps since birth, the grand finale of a situation that had eventually become unbearable.

The next day neither his father nor his brother had gone looking for him. They must have been pleased that he'd fucked off. He phoned them a month later, from the north of France, saying he wasn't planning to come back, that their lives had definitively parted ways. The big world was his home now. Did they get that? He'd practiced his speech in front of a mirror in the pension, jittery as a bandit preparing for the last shoot-out, but, with the phone in his hand, his voice started to quaver. After the indifference with which his father and brother received his news, their nonchalant acceptance of it, the gulf was even greater. "All right. Good luck, then." If Mother was still alive . . . But his mother had died some years earlier, when he was fourteen, and maybe her sudden absence was the first symptom of the whole thing.

———

In bed, before going to sleep, Gori thought about his brother. It wasn't difficult to picture him writing the letter, all alone in his office. Or perhaps after getting home from a session of dialysis. A specialist at the private clinic had spoken to him about his options, had asked if he had siblings. Gori imagined him grabbing the piece of paper in a fit of need and scribbling the words without thinking much about them, as if the gesture was enough to cut through all the years of silence and bring him close. Giving Gori no alternative. Hell, he was his goddamn brother after all. That first-person, future continuous tense—*I'll be needing*—was so imperious that it could only be read ironically. As if gazing into his eyes from the sheet of paper, his brother was saying, "I should be more elegant and ask you politely, but I know you know I'm not like that, that I won't have changed, not even in a moment of despair. If I'm polite and say please help me, you'll see me as false and brown-nosing, and you'll despise me. So, if I ask from my high-handed sense of superiority, you'll see me as I am, your blood brother, and you'll know I'm being sincere and not just arrogant."

In fact, all this could be picked up in his brother's handwriting, in the fractious strokes. He'd always been like that. When they were eleven and twelve, they played together and didn't fight much. Often, if their games in the street led to problems, they'd join forces against some other kid. Gori was a little scrawnier, more reserved. In the playground at school, his big brother had stood up for him more than once. There was an instinctively protective bond between them. Then, one June, their parents decided that his brother was old enough to go off to summer camp and they enrolled him with a group of Boy Scouts. Two weeks in the forest, contact with nature, sleeping in tents, swimming in an icy-cold stream, and discovering the noble savage within. As for Gori, his parents said he'd have to learn to play by himself and smarten up. And if it was a good experience, they could both go the following year.

His brother was excited when he heard the news and soon started planning how he'd fill that space of freedom. His parents bought him a water bottle, a compass, a sleeping bag, and a Swiss Army knife. Gori listened, fiddled with all these things, and longed to go, too. When his brother returned two weeks later, he was different. More distant and serious, he didn't seem to have spent a fortnight camping in the mountains but more as if he'd been dumped all alone on a desert island, struggling to survive against the elements. You'd think he'd been forced to cross some forbidden threshold, to skin a rabbit with his teeth or enter a bat-infested cave.

This new character, moreover, contrasted with Gori's more ingenuous news. In order not to feel so alone in those two weeks, he'd made up an imaginary friend who went everywhere with him. Gori had given him a strange name: Amida. You didn't have to be a genius to see that it was an anagram of his brother's name. Gori and Amida were inseparable. At the swimming pool they jumped off the springboard, the two of them, hand in hand. They read the same *Cavall Fort* magazines together, laughing at the same jokes. Gori also got into the habit of writing in a diary every night before going to sleep. He jotted down what he'd been doing during the day without too many flourishes but always from Amida's point of view: *Day eight without Damià. Today Gori and I had a lemon Popsicle. Then we watched TV and saw the 5,000 meters in the World Athletics Championships.* That kind of stuff. Amida's words, written in real ink, made the invented existence more credible.

His big brother didn't take long to get jealous of Amida. As the elitist effect of his days at the camp wore off and the real-world hierarchy was once again imposed—mother, father, big brother, pesky little brother—he found the invisible kid more and more obnoxious. The first day, while they were having dinner, Gori told him about this incorporeal being and his brother was condescending. *Kids' stuff,* he told himself, and, suddenly adult, caught his father's eye, looking for complicity with a scornful expression. But after a few days he understood that Amida was coming between them. Gori no longer obeyed him like he used to. His power had weakened; his little brother had learned to fill in his time alone—well, not alone but in the company of that idiot Amida; and he felt betrayed, unappreciated, useless. One night, when Gori had gone to sleep, his brother very quietly got up, took the diary and a ballpoint pen, and locked himself in the toilet. After reading a few random entries, full of rage and taking Amida's role for the first and only time, he scribbled on the last page, *I've had a bellyful of Gori today. He's so boring. He's a crybaby. I don't want to see him anymore. I'm getting out of here before daylight. Bye-bye, stupid family!*

The next morning he waited in bed till Gori woke up. They slept in the same room, and on the floor between the two beds lay the diary. Gori saw it immediately, picked it up, smoothed the crumpled pages, and, as if guided by instinct, went straight to the last written page. As he read it, he recognized his brother's crabby script, leapt out of bed, and threw himself on top of him. He'd pay for this. His brother soon overpowered him and, grabbing him by the scruff of the neck with one hand as they'd shown him in the camp, took control, telling him, "I think it's very clear now that this Amida is a jerk. He doesn't deserve to be your friend, Gori. So now we're going to burn this book and then he'll be gone forever."

The two of them went out into the garden, still in pajamas, and, with the help of a little ethanol, burnt the notebook on the barbecue, page by page. Gori, resigned, meek as a lamb, couldn't stop staring at the burning pages, watching how they rose for a few seconds into the air and then fell apart in flakes of ash, like low-flying birds of ill omen.

In his bed, Gori now woke with a start, gasping, with the sensation that a crow's wing had just brushed his cheek. He touched his face because it felt as if he were wearing a mask. He realized that the scene from the past had crept into his dream. Only it wasn't a dream. All those years ago, the pages of his diary had been burnt to a cinder, and his big brother had played the overlord as he fed them into the flames. The memory of his brother who now needed a kidney lay heavy on him again but didn't keep him awake. As he slipped back into oblivion, there was just time for a sketchy thought to form. Why didn't he remember any other episode from his childhood with this clarity? It was as if some anthologist had chosen precisely that awful day to represent the years they'd spent together.

———

The second letter came a week later, with the word *Urgent* written on the envelope. Since he'd known from the very first moment how he'd have to respond to his brother, Gori took cruel pleasure in this new attempt. He was reading the same handwriting, of course, but, on closer scrutiny, perhaps the words written with the impatience he knew so well gave out a jumpier feeling. He spent a couple of minutes toying with the idea of throwing the letter away without opening it or getting the postman to send it back. ADDRESS UNKNOWN, they'd stamp on the envelope. He weighed it in his hand; it seemed thicker than the first one. Curiosity won and he ripped it open. What a letdown! Inside was a sheet of paper with exactly the same sentence: *I'll be needing a kidney*. His brother might be successful but he never had much imagination. The letter looked like a photocopy of the first one. If he'd kept it, Gori would have taken the two sheets of paper, put them together, and looked at them against the light. The only difference he could see was that this time the letter was signed with the initial *D*.

He took from the envelope another check made out to the bearer. Twelve thousand euros. Aha, so he was upping the ante. His brother thought the whole thing was a matter of money . . . Gori was about to tear up the new check as well, but then he thought again. What if he cashed it? He had no debts, but he wasn't loaded either. He couldn't go throwing money around. The problem was that his brother would know. He didn't like the idea that he might turn up some day to reclaim something.

In those thirty years they'd never seen each other in person, either by appointment or by chance. After leaving home, Gori had lived for a while in the village in northern France. In the beginning he'd done simple odd jobs that didn't require much knowledge of the language: for example, being employed as a drudge in a scruffy hotel or working in a garden center where they grew herbs and medicinal plants. The next summer he moved south, joining up with a friend to go grape picking in the Rhône Valley and then, thanks to the advice of an overseer with whom he got on well, he went to live in a village in Roussillon, in the Pyrenean foothills. His French was improving and, moreover, some of the locals spoke Catalan. At first, every time he looked at the huge bulk of the mountains rising before him, he saw it as an impassable wall separating him from his father, his brother, and his country. Over time, the hard feelings diminished and eventually subsided into indifference. The power of inertia in ordinary days, his work as a gardener—which had gradually become his true vocation—and a series of sentimental attachments meant that he'd put down roots there. He even applied for French citizenship, which annoyed some of his friends, who thought it was a stupid idea.

———

When anyone asked Gori how come he'd ended up in that village, he tended to get enigmatic. "A girl," he said, and it was true. He didn't like talking about it. He left the question only partly answered so they could think whatever they wanted. If people prodded him for details, he got testy and cut them off saying it was a "tragic story," which was also true. But it wasn't the girl's fault. If anything, she was the main victim. What happened was this: When Gori was seventeen, he'd started hanging out with a girl in his class. She was a mixed-up kid called Mireia. She and Gori were close and liked being together, often without needing many words. But outside their own little stronghold, Mireia was riding a roller coaster of emotions. She was an only child from a very conservative family, with parents who criticized her about everything, so rebellion was the only state of mind which made her feel alive. More than once when she met up with Gori after some family crisis, exhausted, with red eyes and hands shaking with all the tension, she tearfully told him, "I'm so desperate to grow up!" Upon which he tenderly embraced her.

Meanwhile, Gori's big brother had started college. Economics. Their father had told him that if he finished the degree with good results, he'd leave him the family business and a tidy little sum to expand it. It only took six months of living in a Barcelona student residence for his big brother to turn into a pompous loudmouth, a crashing bore. Now, as well as studying like crazy and playing on the faculty rugby team, he was hanging out with a few scions of Barcelona's haute-bourgeoisie. They had family names that, pronounced at the table during Sunday lunch, made his father's eyes shine with admiration. Gori, however, listening to all this bullshit, was reminded of the other transformation six years earlier, when his brother had come back from camp a lone-wolf predator.

One Saturday night around that time, Mireia came to get Gori at home, and there she found his big brother. Gori had gone to play indoor soccer and still hadn't come back. When he got home half an hour later, the two of them were getting along like a house on fire, laughing, smoking, and drinking beer. Suddenly, against that backdrop, Mireia seemed like another person. Gori never found out what they'd been talking about because neither of them wanted to tell him: "Just stupid things. We were killing time."

After that Saturday, Gori's brother started asking about Mireia. If she and Gori were going out at night to play foos-ball or hitch to the next town, he joined them without ask-ing if he could. He now had his driver's license and offered to take them wherever they wanted to go. The first time Gori sat in front and Mireia behind, but it wasn't long before she asked if she could have the passenger seat so she could choose the music. Then Gori curled up in the back, feeling devoured by the night, concentrating on the sinister songs of The Cure so he wouldn't have to listen to the conversa-tion the two of them were having there in front of him, his brother's exploits in Barcelona and all his insinuations. They were never anything more than stupid, banal stories, but he seemed worldlier now that he lived in the city, and Mireia hung on his every word as if he was giving her a marvelous gift. And, yes, this was making her feel more grown-up. If they went to a bar, Gori drank beer as usual but Mireia imitated his brother and asked for Bombay gin and tonic.

From Monday to Friday, Gori enjoyed having some time to recover lost ground after school. Mireia was attentive again, as if predisposed by the classroom and note-taking atmosphere. They went to the music shop to listen to songs with headphones, new releases by Ultravox, Depeche Mode, and Japan. They laughed and shouted till the salesclerk told them off. They wandered round the park, kissed, felt each other up, and then he walked her home. If he sometimes hinted that they could take the sex a bit further—at his place they'd be alone—she always found excuses. Wanted to, wouldn't do. She was scared of her parents.

One afternoon, as they were talking, she casually let it drop that Gori's brother had phoned her from Barcelona. Gori snorted with rage.

"It's no big deal," she said, trying to calm him. "I know your brother's full of himself."

"But do you like him?" he asked.

"I don't know. I like you both . . . But I think I like you more."

Another day, after school, Mireia told Gori that his brother had phoned and invited them to go to Barcelona.

"He said we could go by train on Saturday afternoon and he'll bring us back by car later on at night. What do you think? We wouldn't be home too late. It'll be like a normal Saturday. I'll make up some excuse for my folks, like I'm studying for the exams with some girlfriends . . ."

Her voice had a ring of unconscious pleading. Gori forced a smile and said he'd think about it, but he was sure it couldn't happen. What an asshole his brother was. He knew perfectly well that Gori had to play a decisive soccer game that Saturday.

In the end, Mireia went to Barcelona alone. When Gori's brother dropped her home early in the morning with her feelings in turmoil, her parents were waiting up for her with a whole arsenal of accusations and reproaches. They made such a fuss that they only aggravated the emotional mess she was in, which was bad enough already. In a fit of inconsolable weeping, she left them still railing at her and locked herself in her room. Midmorning the next day, Gori roughly woke his brother.

"So, did you and Mireia have fun?" He was trying to sound sarcastic. His brother gave him a malicious smirk, which said everything, but went on to inform him that things couldn't go on as they had been.

"Last night, Gori, when I left Mireia at her place, I told her she has to choose for once and for all. You or me. She's playing with us and I'm fed up with humoring her. You get it? If she prefers you, fine. I'll find another girl. If she chooses me, you do the same."

That afternoon Gori phoned Mireia but couldn't speak to her. "I don't know what you two did to her yesterday"— her father was really worked up—"but one thing's for sure: you and your brother will never see her again. Assholes!"

The uncertainty dragged on for a while, as if some outside power was pushing all of them into the inevitable rural drama. At school, during the week, Gori could see that Mireia was off in another world and was ignoring him. She did things automatically, carrying on as if he weren't there or as if someone were forcing her not to notice him, because if she did, things would only get worse. On Saturdays, when his brother came back from Barcelona, her parents were more watchful than ever and found excuses to stop her from going out: a family dinner, a visit to some cousins who lived far away . . . As tends to happen, the results of this blocking tactic were the opposite of what they wanted, and Gori's brother's ultimatum—"him or me"—was taking on terrible dimensions, becoming the unendurable suffocation of intergenerational strife. And one Monday evening while her parents were out shopping, unable to decide or know what she wanted, Mireia got in the bathtub and slit her wrists.

Two days after that, Gori went to the funeral. And left home forever.

——

Gori received his brother's third letter a week later. His name and address were written in the same hand but this time there was no stamp on the envelope. Someone had come and dropped it through his letterbox. Gori opened the door and looked out into the street but saw no one who might be the mysterious postman. Whatever the case, it was unimaginable that his brother would have come there to ask him for a kidney. Inside the envelope, the text was a little different this time: *I really need a kidney, Gregori. It's very urgent now. It has to be one of yours. Tell me what you want.* The check, made out to the bearer, confirmed the desperation, because no figure was written: *Write it yourself, Gori.*

In thirty years of exile from his family, Gori had received direct news of his brother on three occasions, once per decade. The first time was when his father died, just three years after he'd left, and instead of making him sad, it made him even surer of the decision he'd taken. The family lawyer had moved heaven and earth to find his address in the South of France, only to give him a will certifying that he wasn't getting anything except the legitim, a pathetic amount, because, before his death, his father had given everything to his big brother.

One day, more than a decade earlier, he'd had a surprise visit from a Barcelona journalist. This was the second time Gori had news of his brother. It turned out that, at the age of only thirty-five, he'd been appointed to a big job: CEO of an innovative electronics company. The newspaper had just chosen him as its business "revelation of the year," and the journalist was writing a profile. In his hometown, the lawyer had told him about Gori, "the distant brother," and now the journalist had come to see him because he was interested in his character's rough edges. In the world of business, there's no winner who hasn't left enemies along the way, he said. Gori was polite but told him he had nothing to say. He didn't let him take photos either. Since the journalist kept pressing, he finally said that he and his brother had simply gone their separate ways when they were young.

He felt no rancor or anything like that. No affection either. Over the years, the blood relationship that had once united them had shrunk into nothing more than a mere whimsy of chance.

The journalist left disappointed, but, in the end, these few words had given some critical balance to an excessively laudatory article. Gori read it in the bar one Saturday morning and came to two conclusions. First, he liked being the black sheep of the family, and, second, his brother had aged much worse than he had. Despite the tan he was sporting in the photos, years of constant damage control and bluster had taken their toll.

Thanks to the journalist's profile, a lot of people discovered that the great D, man of the moment, had a younger brother. This is what happened with his two daughters who'd never heard of an Uncle Gori. The younger one was the cause of the third occasion Gori had news of his brother. Five years earlier, unknown to her father, she took the occasion of a holiday in the South of France to go and meet her runaway uncle. One morning in August, Gori opened the door to find a girl who looked a lot like his mother. He was dumbfounded! His niece set about trying to bond with Gori by badmouthing her father—a despot, she said. Ever since she'd first heard of him, he'd become a legend for her, the image of freedom she summoned up whenever she was trying to escape from family pressures. Once, in the middle of an argument with her father, she'd said, "One day I'm going to get away, like my uncle did!" Then he really read her the riot act.

Gori didn't pay too much attention to his niece's words, although deep down he felt smug. He was dismayed that his long-gone past should crop up again so unexpectedly, but he also told himself that, if it had to happen, it was better like that, in the form of the girl's rebellion. When they said goodbye, he promised her they'd phone from time to time, or at least he'd return her calls. But then, when the time came, he didn't. It would have felt like betraying himself.

The day Gori received the third letter, someone knocked at his door in the evening. Opening it, he saw his niece.

"Hi, Uncle Gori. Can I come in?"

She'd delivered the letter and now she'd come to ask him to help her father. She believed she was the only family tie between the two of them and, feeling this strongly, thought she had to try. Her father's condition was worsening. It was no joke. He really needed a kidney, so please forget about his arrogance. Gori heard her out without a single interruption. He felt relieved. This had been going on too long. If it was amusing in the beginning, now it was getting annoying. When the girl went quiet, he finally gave her the answer he'd been savoring all along.

"Tell your father I'm sorry but I can't give him a kidney. I've only got one," he said. "I had surgery a year and a half ago. Must be genetic."

CONSOLATION PRIZE

An Analogical Tale

He lets the dog off its leash, whereupon it madly rushes up and down, from one tree to another, capering about and rolling in the damp grass. It's almost midnight and, at this hour, cool in the park. The sensation of solitude is heightened because it's almost deserted and the only sound is the disciplined swishing of a distant sprinkler. Now and then, at the end of one of the narrow paths around which the park is structured, he can make out the silhouette of a pedestrian taking a shortcut on the way home, or the shadow of some night-owl smoker sitting all alone on a bench. It's quite a discreet park with no bars fencing it off and the surrounding streets are some distance away, sufficiently hidden for him not to have to worry about the safety of the six-month-old truly kamikaze pup.

It's not even a month since Ibon adopted him. One

afternoon after work, not yet totally convinced, he went to the municipal dog pound. Checking out the cages amid a chorus of mournful whines and howls, he noticed that he was being watched by the doleful eyes of a small mongrel with a coat of different burnt umber tones (which is probably why he called it Whisky). He immediately saw himself reflected there, the same forlorn expression of a man adrift, which had been petrifying on his face for some time now. It was as if the sedentary life he led totally naturally, without complications but also without major happiness, had decided to sound an alarm.

Ibon chooses a bench in the park and sits down, keeping an eye on the giddy pup. He calls him from time to time and Whisky obediently trots over for a few seconds but then sniffs out something and is off again. The scene wouldn't be remarkable if another dog hadn't appeared just then, a weary, old, slow-moving German shepherd with his owner ambling along behind him with the same listless air. Maybe dogs and their owners do end up resembling each other over time. The stranger (but Ibon will soon discover that he's called Emili) stops under a lamppost and lights a cigarette. He's taking his time and, as he goes past Ibon—perhaps prompted by the involuntarily furtiveness of the encounter—stops to say hello. With an automatic gesture, Ibon pulls out his earphones and turns off his Walkman (putting an end to muffled crackling noises) and says hello back. Emili sits on the bench. Without forcing things, they exchange a few pleasantries about dogs and then introduce themselves. Ibon, Emili, plus a series of increasingly personal questions and answers fill ten minutes of conversation. They both live in the neighborhood, go to the same supermarket (but have never seen each other as far as they can recall), and read the same newspaper (but buy it in different newsstands, equidistant from the park).

Then Emili says, "And you like soccer." It's more a statement than a question.

"No, not especially," says Ibon. "What makes you say that?"

"Your radio. I thought you were listening to one of those sports programs with offensive yelling commentators and all the rest. They're very popular now."

"No, not sports. I always listen to music. It's a Walkman." He shows it to Emili. "I like walking the dog and listening to songs I've known for ages. Sometimes I record tapes for particular situations. Like this one. It's for coming to walk in the park at midnight." He pauses, wondering if he should say what he wants to say, and the absence of personal ties emboldens him. "Sometimes . . . sometimes, if I'm alone here, I listen to a song and imagine I'm making a clip of it. I must have an actor inside me, you know, because I often want to play the part of what the words in a song are saying."

Emili smiles and tries to hide his bemusement but says nothing. Now they're silent as they're trying to see where their dogs are. They're nearby. Boris, the German shepherd, is lying quietly on the grass, indifferent to the frolickings of Whisky, who keeps bounding over to him, trying to tempt him to play.

"I'm very conventional when it comes to music. Too much so, probably, I admit," Emili says finally. "I like the hits of the season, the typical stuff you hear all day long on the radio. Then, after a while, I forget them. What were you listening to just now?"

"Yeah, well, as I say, nothing up-to-date. I doubt you'd know them. The thing is, I got stuck in the eighties. The ones I had on just now are some English guys called Orange Juice," Ibon explains. Hearing the name, Emili raises his eyebrows. "I've known their songs by heart for years and I never get sick of them. This one, the one I was just listening to, is really great. It's called 'A Place in My Heart' and it cheers me up."

"Well, I do know Orange Juice. How about that?" Emili's amused. "It's quite a coincidence, but seven or eight years ago I had a girlfriend who was really into them, and she was especially crazy about this song. Since she didn't know English, she asked me to translate the lyrics. 'There'll always be a place in my heart for you . . . ,'" he recalls, without showing the slightest glimmer of nostalgia. "But, to tell you the truth, Orange Juice doesn't do anything for me. They always sounded the same, but I went along with it because I was mad about her and everything she said was fine by me. At the time she was really obsessed with them . . . Who knows, maybe that's why we split in the end. We had very different tastes."

Ibon feels a shiver under his skin, at first unpleasant and then agreeable. The coincidence, so glowing in his eyes, seems to be the recognition of some kind of biased alliance, with the balance tipped by someone who's come between them. He feels strange, as if the scene were dreamed up some time ago by somebody else—written down, even— and now it only has to be acted out. So he shamelessly asks Emili the name of the woman who was enamored of Orange Juice. Emili smirks slyly and he, too, says what he must say.

"Anna, her name was Anna Fuguet, but it's been years since I had any news of her." He goes quiet for a moment, as if trying to summon up her face, good and bad memories suddenly awakening, and then he says, "Life's strange, huh? I guess you should have met her instead of me."

It's late. They're cold sitting there. They get up, call the dogs, attach their leashes, and say goodbye, confirming that they'll see each other again for sure, here in the park some-day.

———

On his way home with Whisky, Ibon winds the tape back three times to listen to the Orange Juice song and each time it sounds new. Now, with this latent input from the unknown Anna, he gets goose bumps more than once, remembering how he felt in those early days when he was fascinated by those satiny trumpets, the inlays on James Kirk's guitar, the joyful, mocking voice of Edwyn Collins, and imagining this Anna (still faceless) ten or twelve years back, the whole Anna—also muzzy—levitating as she heard the song for the first time, after which she mentally repeated it over and over again like a wholesome mantra.

Half an hour later, now at home, Ibon goes to bed and, lying there in the dark, listens to the song once more. He's hoping it will filter into his sleep like a narcotic to become the soundtrack of his dreams, a fabulous movie, but in fact he drops off to sleep immediately and doesn't dream about Anna.

The next day his alarm clock installs him yet again in the hyperactivity disorder of his daily routine, and, once out of bed, he robotically performs his morning ritual. When he pulls up the blanket to give the impression that the bed is made, he finds the Walkman hidden in the recesses of a cave made by his pillow and the sheet but doesn't wonder how it got there. Neither does he look for any particular trace of his conversation with Emili last night, and not even the sight of Whisky lying in his corner makes him think about the state he was in before he went to sleep. When he's shaving, however, something special happens, and this is worth recalling. He lathers the shaving cream over his chin and cheeks and then, without looking in the mirror, scrapes the razor along its usual tracks. When he thinks it's necessary he rinses it under the tap and then marks out a new path in the foam. But now his hand slips and he cuts himself just above his upper lip, a neat, surgical, painless slash. He moves closer to the mirror and sees that it's bleeding a little. He squeezes the edges together with his fingers and sees that the blood's flowing past the corner of his mouth and down to his chin. He licks it, trying to stop it—noting the plastic taste of the foam—but three dense round drops of blood escape and drop onto the white marble of the sink. The blood is then partly diluted by the drops of water already there, and the mingling liquids somehow sketch the features of a face, natural in color, fleshy looking, red on white. Ibon is absorbed in his contemplation of the image. He loses himself in it. He believes he's discovered a portrait of the clear, beautiful features of Anna Fuguet.

That evening, after dinner in front of the TV set, Ibon is even more impatient than Whisky to go out and walk in the park. The prospect of another meeting with Emili has incredible appeal. Like an emblem of his new yearning, Anna's recently outlined face has been with him all day long and has been growing into a dangerous, mythical, unattainable presence. He needs to put an end to this, and the sooner the better. He's desperate to get some detail that will put her in the real world, in the same city, some clue that will make her tangible, carnal, sexual, and Emili is the only person who can supply this information. He heads for the park earlier than usual and starts strolling around, keeping the dog on the leash and wondering whether it might not be better to go directly to the same bench they sat on yesterday. Because of some strange superstition he hasn't brought the Walkman, and without music in his ears he has the sensation that time has slowed down, that the silence in the park is congealing and becoming almost aggravating. He tries to distract himself by looking at the quiet pattern of sleeping trees and flowers, trash cans, shop signs on the other side of the street, windows of apartment blocks lit up among the foliage, and finally he hears a voice calling his name. It's Emili. They greet one another and repeat platitudes about dogs with the odd variant, but Emili wastes no time in doing his bit to calm Ibon's agitation, which is evident in his face.

"You want to know more about Anna, huh? I got you intrigued yesterday."

Ibon nods. He's moved by hearing another person pronouncing the name, because it makes her more alive, more present.

"We called it a day six or seven years back," Emili says, "and the last time I updated my phone book contacts I didn't make a note of her number. But I recall a few things: I know where she was working and what she was doing then—real estate—remember that she wanted to move out of her apartment, and that she liked silent movie comedies: I gave her a poster with that image of Harold Lloyd hanging from the hands of a clock. And I remember what she was like, of course, but that would be more difficult for me to explain, because it's mainly sensations. I can only say that it was a long time ago, that we didn't end well, but now that you've made me think about her again, I realize that my memory of her has been getting warmer and more attractive. Some people have that virtue, don't they? They know how to live without making a fuss about anything."

He still needs more details, he needs everything, but instead of feeling let down, Ibon clings to what there is with the instinct and tenacity of a newborn babe. He listens to Emili's reminiscences—which are precise but, for all that, insubstantial—and avidly commits them to memory. He asks lots of questions, which Emili answers good-humoredly for the pure pleasure of reviving the Anna of those days, like someone recalling some especially madcap adolescent vacations. No—and this is incomprehensible—there are no photos of Anna. Yes, he's seen her again a couple of times, in the distance and, oddly enough, in the neighborhood, but then, as he recalls, her parents lived nearby. Yes, he could say that back then, when he met her—it lasted only a year, so no worries, OK—she was attractive, slightly melancholy (sometimes she cried for no reason at all), and she had a special gleam in her eyes, which were a greenish blue, two wild grottos you wanted to dive into, believe me. And yes, yes, she loved Orange Juice. Oh, yeah, she was mad about them, and it wasn't just one song but all of them. She venerated them, was almost snobbish about it, with the pride of belonging to a select club.

Emili's last words make Ibon more desperate to meet Anna. She's becoming less hazy every second and he's certain that he has to meet her right now. He can't wait. Not even a day. She must become his center of gravity. With his heart racing out of control, he says good night to Emili, who notes, with a touch of envy, this crazy desire he's triggered. Ibon wants to get home as fast as he can and listen to Orange Juice again, trying to find some clue, striving to imagine the emotions, the agitation, and the experiences that she—oh, she, divine stranger, distant love—must have associated with each song, and, finally, he wants Anna to appear before him, taking shape as an increasingly perfect hologram, like Princess Leia, and to stay by his side and never ever leave him.

When they part ways, Emili has a sudden attack of fright—well, not exactly fright, but more like apprehension—and feels the need to call out. Ibon turns around.

"Ibon, hey, I guess you'll tell me if you find her," Emili says. Ibon snickers nervously. "Don't forget, it's a long time since I last saw her. Everything might have changed."

"No, no, I don't think so. I'm sure it hasn't," Ibon shouts elatedly, and then lets himself be pulled along by the innocent haste of Whisky, who keeps straining at his lead.

———

For Ibon, the next few hours that night are either a mortification he craves or an irritating balm, but what they unleash in the end is worth telling here. Most people have a predictable life, more or less set in stone, and chance alone—but only sometimes—holds out the opportunity to change and revamp it. This is often just a fleeting mirage, and things soon go back to being what they were; but this sense of being unmoored is so seductive that it's not such a bad idea to be tempted, to see where it leads, even if it's going nowhere. It must be said, then, that until dawn almost all the songs of Orange Juice stream nonstop from Ibon's Walkman. As he listens to them and, full of emotion, sings them in his heart, he thinks again about what Emili said about Anna, and in his head the music and the images turn into a hopelessly tangled amalgam, the convincing result of an impossible exercise in archaeology of the future.

He recalls that Emili said he'd bumped into Anna a couple of times in the neighborhood, and then it dawns on him that he might have seen her without knowing it, perhaps sitting next to her having a coffee in a bar, or buying bread, two strangers who chance has decided aren't going to come together, no, not yet, and he's immediately invaded by a feeling of regret for those wasted moments. After a sad song by Orange Juice he gets alarmed because the song seems to hint that Anna might be dead. Why not? There's nothing to contradict the idea. Maybe she died months ago, in a traffic accident. Who knows? Or maybe that very afternoon, when he was coming home from work on the subway, uselessly checking out the women surrounding him in his coach. Or maybe she's very ill and dying right now while he's thinking these things. For a few seconds he's swamped in fathomless sadness, and just when he's about to surrender to it, annihilated with no hope of recovery, there's a silence, then another song starts and it saves him. It's "Consolation Prize" and, as the words suggest, he'd willingly be Anna's consolation prize. And now he imagines her, very clearly, in slow-motion camera. He hears her happy, buoyant laughter as he listens to "I Guess I'm Just a Little Too Sensitive." She's in someone's apartment, sitting in a chair with a beer in her hand, people all around her, and she's smoking, drinking, and talking with her friends, but he can also see her slowly keeping time with her head, her eyes gradually going glassy, staring at some indefinite point, some point in the future, and he's there waiting for her. The world around her evaporates and only Anna remains.

Caught up in this delirium, Ibon is so tired, he goes to sleep on the sofa. He wakes up a couple of hours later feeling cold. It's another day, and he gets up to go to the toilet. He wets his face and hair and then, still not fully awake, calls the office and tells the receptionist that he's not well today and won't be coming in to work. As for tomorrow, he'll have to wait and see. It depends. When he hangs up, he returns to the bathroom and goes very close to the mirror. He needs to return to the liquid portrait of Anna, profiled against the marble sink. With his finger he traces the small cut of the previous day, next to his upper lip, and starts squeezing it, trying to open it up again. That's not difficult, but the wound must be healing, because he can't get a single drop of blood. Nevertheless, in the gradually revealed pulpy, purplish flesh, he can discern Anna's silky, lustful sex, opening up for him and for him alone, and he has to masturbate right then and there.

———

Not hungry and picking at his breakfast, he leafs through the previous Sunday's newspaper, looking for real estate ads. He remembers the name of the agency Emili mentioned and wants to reassure himself that Anna's still working there, even though so many years have gone by. He flips quickly through the pages without really looking and realizes that the headlines he's glimpsing out of the corner of his eye seem remote, standard, as if, instead of having survived three days and that's all, half a life has slipped away from him because she wasn't at his side. So he begins to rip up the newspaper, crumpling the pages to make a ball, which he throws on the floor for Whisky to play with. But when he gets to the real estate pages he sets about examining the columns of tiny letters, the repetitive, specious phrases of housing market literature. He pores over them obsessively until his head is spinning. Even so, it's not difficult for him to find the agency's logo or an apartment for sale not far away and at a reasonable price for his illusory hopes. *I have nothing to lose,* he tells himself. His heart missing a beat, he dials the number in the ad and asks for information about the apartment. The switchboard operator tells him to wait a moment and forwards the call to an agent. A woman answers (but she doesn't sound as if her name is Anna), singing the praises of that high, sunny apartment, with great views. It's a gem, believe me, she says. He's anxious, nodding all the while, yeah, hmm, yeah, and perhaps he's a little too quick to ask if they can show it to him, because he really wants to see it. The few details she's offered have given him good vibes—and that's exactly what he said, "good vibes," as if to encourage himself. Yes, certainly. Of course. They can meet tomorrow morning. But couldn't it be today, late afternoon? Tomorrow doesn't really suit him. Ibon's quivering with impatience. He'd bite all his nails if his hands and mouth weren't already occupied. The woman hesitates for a moment—three or four seconds, maybe— and he can hear pages of an agenda being turned in the background. Then she says OK, six o'clock will be all right, the last appointment of the day. She asks him to jot down the exact address. Hearing this, Ibon is relieved but grips the phone tighter when he thanks her. Now there's only one matter left to sort out, the most important thing, so, somewhat agitated, he hears himself saying, "Excuse me, but there's just one more question." Now he's getting ready to lie. "About five or six years ago, when I rented the apartment where I live now, it was handled by a very nice agent. I think her name was Anna . . . Anna Fuguet?"

"Oh, right, that's me," says Anna in a voice that is nothing like the one he imagined. Then she lets out a giggle that could be either playful or incredulous, confirms that she'll see him at six this afternoon, and hangs up.

———

Ibon, however, takes almost four minutes to hang up. Standing there in a silence interrupted only by beeps from the phone, he hears Anna's words harmoniously echoing over and over again in his head, swelling with that laugh, which he knows was one of deep understanding, coming from a long way back. Yes, that was her voice. How silly of him to have doubted it: it was gorgeous, musical, friendly, welcoming. The portrait is more and more positive, his senses increasingly fine-tuned, and he can't believe he's going to meet her and will be able to talk to her in just a few hours.

At this point, the narrator would like to skip the details of Ibon's enervating wait. The hands of the clock keep dawdling all day long, filling his afternoon with doubts. *What to wear? Shall I take a novel in case she arrives late? Should I start talking about Orange Juice immediately? Do I need to mention Emili? (Definitely not!)* It's all unnecessary anyway, because destiny does its job of shepherding the hours and the meeting is definitely arranged. So let's go.

It's nearly six and Ibon is more than punctual when he arrives at the address he's been given. All day long, after hanging up the phone, he's planned with the meticulousness of a movie director (and some hysteria) how the first instant of his life with Anna will be played out—the looks, the gestures, the angles from which the cameras will film the imaginary scene; but, as it happens, Anna ignores the script and improvises. Ibon is looking up and down the sidewalk, gazing at the faces of passersby and expecting to see a woman coming toward him with an air of knowing what she's doing. Then he hears the street door of the building opening behind him and a voice saying hello.

"You must be Ibon," says Anna. He turns, startled, flabbergasted, says yes, and shyly holds out his hand. She's finally standing there before him, alive, complete, defined, and their eyes meet for the first time. Once he's over the initial astonishment, he relaxes—from her saleswoman's experience, she's silently grateful for this—and now, for an intense tenth of a second, Ibon contemplates the whole Anna in all her splendor. Yes, in essence it's the same face he divined at home outlined on marble, but with one small difference. The real Anna has her hair pulled back, which is probably required for her saleswoman's image. Ibon lets the momentary dissonance melt away into the agitation of the present and asks how come she was upstairs in the apartment. She says she went up to open the windows and air it, as it's been closed up for a while and is a little stuffy, as he'll notice. Then she invites him to come up. She's not sure if she told him by phone, but it's on the sixth floor and very sunny.

For Ibon, the elevator is a decompression chamber. Locked inside it with Anna, the two of them in that tiny space, he soon understands that he mustn't rush things, that he has to play his part, be guided by her, and see what happens. He asks her about the neighbors, how old the building is, and if anyone else has a dog (he has a six-month-old pup called Whisky, an adorable little fellow). Inside the apartment, the ceremony of walking around empty rooms begins. Anna, very professional, first shows him where each one is and draws attention to their qualities: spacious dining room, practical kitchen, very quiet bedrooms—two of them—and a fully fitted bathroom. They go out for a moment onto the small terrace, where two flowerpots full of dry earth have survived and, using the same words, they both praise the view of the city and the green of the trees in the nearby park, just four or five streets away. Some people would pay a fortune for this view. Then she leaves him so he can look around by himself and think it over. Meanwhile, she sits on the only chair in the dining room, a wobbly bit of junk that someone separated from its family, and consults her agenda to organize her appointments for tomorrow.

For all his excitement, Ibon immediately sees that the apartment is pretty ordinary, but he pretends he likes it so he can spend a little longer with her. He goes back into every empty room, listening to his footsteps echoing in the silence of the evening. A vague melancholy floats around the apartment, slipping through walls where dust has framed ghosts of former furniture, mirrors, and pictures. Yet he doesn't think it's a gloomy melancholy. Maybe that's why he starts humming "A Place in My Heart," his fetish song by Orange Juice, and he can't help filling up the emptiness with snippets of his future life. He's totally unembarrassed about fancying that he's living here with Anna. He goes into the kitchen and clearly sees the two of them having breakfast in the morning before leaving for work. He's in somewhat of a hurry and playfully dunks his muffin in her latte. She pretends she's annoyed. He laughs until he's got globs of wet muffin shooting out of his nose. Then they both laugh even more. In one of the rooms, their bedroom, he witnesses the final touching notes of a scene where they're sitting on the bed, making up after a ridiculous squabble and, all of a sudden, he feels like a little boy, the son who doesn't quite understand but knows he's happy because Mommy and Daddy love each other again. He returns to the dining room and, from the passage, seeing the real, physical Anna outlined against the slanting evening sunlight, stops humming Orange Juice. He sneaks up closer and leans in the doorway without going into the room. You could say that here, too, Ibon is mentally starring in some corny video. He watches her concentrating on her papers, radiant, her hair tied back. A movement of her lips, which he finds sensual, seems to promise many things. She's not aware of his presence. Carried away by the mystery of the scene, he spontaneously closes his eyes as if asking for a wish, constructing a fantasy in the space there before him. *Look, here we are and we're feeling cold. We're on the sofa, snuggled up together. We're watching a silent movie on TV, giggling more and more because it's so funny. From time to time you whisper things in my ear, you tickle me, and I tenderly caress you. I wish you could feel how my heart's beating for you, a metronome you set off* . . .

"So, what do you think, Ibon? Do you like the apartment?"

Anna's words jolt him out of his reverie and back into the real world. He opens his eyes. Still daydreaming, he babbles, Oh, yes, I like it very much and I'm sure that with a coat of paint and new furniture it would gain a lot. Anna agrees. She's convinced of it, and she'd even go so far as to say that in the last few days she's thought more than once that she'd like to buy it for herself, because it's ideal for an independent person like her who lives alone. Alone or with a partner or, yeah, sure, with a dog, too, and she laughs. Ibon's so pleased, he shivers inside and he also laughs. He realizes that it's been a while since he laughed like that—really laughed. While Anna closes the windows again, they talk about the price. It's expensive but negotiable. He says he wants to think about it for a while, ask his bank about a mortgage, and all the rest. She says of course, certainly, and if he wants, they can talk about it again. "Yes, we'll talk about it," she says. "Phone me when you're ready. I can see you're quite tempted." These words, containing the essence of Ibon's future life and almost sounding—almost—like a proposition, spark off in him an amazing flash of self-confidence. So, when they're going down in the elevator (a second decompression phase) he dauntlessly dives in the deep end and asks if she has time for a beer— no big deal, just five minutes—because he wants to know a couple more details about the apartment. Hearing this, she accepts without hesitation and, you might even say, with some enthusiasm.

———

The five minutes multiply into more than an hour. They find a place nearby and go inside. Ibon points at the bar, but Anna says she'd prefer to sit at a table, as she's tired after running around in high heels all day. They ask for a couple of beers and she, wanting to feel more relaxed, loosens her hair. With the same movement as an actress in a period movie, brushing her hair before going to bed, Anna ripples her wavy tresses as if combing out fatigue, and the next thing she does is send an extremely calculated look Ibon's way: brief, stabbing, a whiplash of a look. He finally discovers the dive-into-me, slightly misty green of her eyes and tries to hold her gaze but soon desists. He feels light-headed, so, trying to cover up, he takes a sip of beer and she follows suit. They start talking about the apartment and both of them repeat what they've already said up there. Anna realizes this and tries to steer the conversation onto more personal ground, thus prompting Ibon to try to find a propitious moment to make some reference to Orange Juice. Slowly they start opening up cracks, increasingly trusting, as a whole heap of innocuous and revealing details about their past lives start coming to light. Bait set for mutual attraction.

Things are going well, yes, and Ibon even has the impression that maybe he won't have to raise the subject of Orange Juice—not yet—not today, but then the meanderings of chit-chat present the occasion. They're talking about friendship, getting older, and Anna is telling him that she still sees some of her friends from her high school days a couple of times a year. Their lives are poles apart, and the distance between them has grown with time, but there's something—she doesn't know what exactly, but something related with the past they shared—that keeps them united in their distance.

"The same thing's happened to me with a couple of friends," Ibon lies, "but the difference is that we know what keeps us together."

"And what's that?" Her curiosity is piqued.

"Music. We've got the same tastes and we went to a lot of concerts together. Our favorite band, I'd say, was Orange Juice." Ibon finally pronounces the two words, feeling sure of himself and believing it's time to show his cards. "Sometimes we still meet up in someone's place for retro music sessions. It's embarrassing even to think about. We drink, dance, and we can be really pathetic . . ." He leaves the sentence hanging to see how she'll react, to seek some generational connection, and then he asks, "Do you know them? Orange Juice? Did you like them, by any chance?"

"Yeah, pfft . . . ," she says with surprising indifference. Ibon picks up his empty beer glass and, unaware of what he's doing, nervously fiddles with it. "There was a time when I loved them," she says. "I was mad about them. But one day I stopped listening to them and that was that."

"Why?" he ventures, in a barely audible voice.

"I don't know how to put it. Well, maybe I got bored with them because of a boyfriend I had. He was always a clingy pain in the neck. Or maybe I just grew out of them—simply that. Tastes change over the years. Something inside me, but now I can't identify what, made me forget about them. Who knows: if I listened to them again, I'd most probably want to relive that time of my life, but only for five minutes. I'm not at all romantic about these things. Now I tend to like the new Van Morrison records, for example."

Anna smiles, shrugs, and takes a sip of beer. Ibon doesn't say anything. He puts his empty glass back on the table and thinks about what she's said. He's not sure whether he should feel shattered or not. He's done what he wanted to do, she's sitting there opposite him, and he feels good about it. He tells himself that this is what counts. He prepares to look up and gaze at her very honestly. He'll do it in a moment. Meanwhile, Anna decides she wants to know more about this stranger who has so self-assuredly walked into her life one run-of-the-mill evening—this stranger who's capable of calling an adopted dog Whisky and openly abandoning himself to his thoughts and feelings, or whatever, with his eyes closed and leaning in a doorway. So when he looks up and into her eyes (right now), she says it's getting late and she must go, but if he likes, they can meet tomorrow. Same time, same place. Ibon smiles, nods, and then says yes, sure.

In the street they say goodbye with cheek kisses and head off in opposite directions. They've taken only a few steps when Anna turns and calls his name as if in the final scene of the video or even a movie, one with a happy ending. Ibon turns, too, right on cue, as if he was waiting for this.

"Hey, now that I think about it," she says, "that song you were humming upstairs when you were walking round the rooms . . . that was Orange Juice, wasn't it?"

"I don't know," says Ibon. "To tell the truth, I don't remember."

MY BEST FRIEND'S MOTHER

The same artificial plants are still there, half-hidden in their corners, leaves made of fabric in greenish tones, and the earth dry. I'm sure that if I went and ran a finger over them, I'd find that they're covered in dust and feel like parchment, because they're so steeped with old smoke, but the green spotlight shining up from underneath makes them gleam with a gush of chlorophyll that looks tremendously authentic. But the carpet's different. They must have changed it a few years ago in one of those hopeful attempts to renovate the place and its clientele, but now it's shabby again, full of stains and pocked with cigarette burns. When I first came in, the stink of wholesale air freshener almost knocked me out; but now I've recovered from that, and everything's giving me a sense of security as if my senses are drugged again after all these years. I have no trouble at all recognizing the smells, the strategic angles, the dark zones where you can lose yourself in company. I turn around from my spot at the bar and confidently take in the whole scene, slowly scanning it, sweeping over it, looking for the points of warmth (her). After all these years—it must be more than twenty—the waiters have changed, the music has changed (but not a lot), and me, too. I'm married, I have a daughter, and I've stopped smoking.

Even after all this time, right now I could close my eyes and move around the place without crashing into anything. I know I'd instinctively start walking toward the dance floor with a long drink in my hand, swaying in time with the music (let's say I was a little cocky), and on the way I'd stop to light a cigarette and so on, but no, no, I haven't come here to revive those falsely dizzying years. I'm here, in the Peculiar, the old pub near Passeig de la Bonanova, at six in the afternoon this Sunday to meet up with her again, Senyora Elsa, her skin, so soft and golden from skiing, the Nordic blue eyes, the straight (and later, when it was in fashion, permed) blond hair. And while I'm looking for her—because I know she'll be here, I know she will—I pray, I hope that we haven't changed much in these two decades, not her and not me, and that one smile will be enough for her to blow me away, as she did then, that one and only time, in another more private place.

Her smile—debauched, as I decided then—topped up my erotic tanks for months on end. They never got depleted. On the contrary, it was a lewd image engraved in my brain where, once installed, it kept growing, flourishing as if my devotion turned her on, too. When I needed her to add some color to my uneasy adolescent's fantasies, Senyora Elsa was always there, delicate and obliging, never protesting, always ready to welcome me and satisfy my desires. Did I want her to take me by the hand and lead me to the bedroom, shedding her clothes along the way? No problem. Inside my head she always did it, and every movement she made was so sexy. And did I want her to caress her nipple and look at me with eyes burning with desire? Of course she would. Delighted!

In fact, it was only the nights in this pub that, with time, managed to make that private Senyora Elsa, my best friend's mother, fade away. Yet, when I came out of the Peculiar with some girl and we got in the car to head off to the Arrabassada road and park in some out-of-the-way flat spot to get into some necking and petting—and even when I finally managed to get laid (because sometimes I did)—Senyora Elsa's voice echoed inside me, slinky, velvety, automatically reminding me, OK, go ahead, but she was still first on the list, number one, the foundational fervor. And that's why—and because my wife is too real to figure on any list (at one point she did, of course, and in a good position)—I went out this Sunday afternoon with the lame excuse of watching a soccer match with friends in some noisy bar and why, when it still wasn't quite dark outside, I came into this pub thinking I had three hours, more or less, to find Senyora Elsa and top up my fantasy tank again, because recently I've needed to.

Sitting at the bar, then, I check out the groups scattered

round the pub. There are more spotlights than there used to be, but it's a fake light and the clients look like wax-work figures. The music helps, too: they're playing songs by Billy Joel, the Eagles, and Dire Straits. On closer scrutiny, it seems I'm still the youngest person here. Prostate-challenged old guys, necks swathed in silk cravats, dodder up to the bar asking for colorful cocktails. Separated women with bone-dry hair sashay their way through the tables with great poise as if they were at home in the dining room, or they sit in the bamboo chairs emanating fairly expensive perfume that is befouled by the air freshener. Some women look at me as if I'm an intruder, peeved because I'm lower-ing the average age, but others—and I can tell—who are more practiced are instinctively gauging the real possibili-ties and they're not letting me out of their sight. From time to time, clear, ringing laughter, the conspicuous kind that can catch fire, rises from some group, or I see slim fingers mechanically playing with the pearls of a necklace and, all at once, I think they belong to Senyora Elsa. Like now, at a table where five women are seated, one of them stands up to show the others some detail of the dress she's wearing today. She's slender, smiling, and she passes her hand over her belly, smoothing out the fabric. Then, saying something I can't hear (but which makes the other ladies laugh), she pulls up her skirt just a little to show muscular thighs that have benefited from the tanning bed and the gym, and her gestures are so pitch-perfect, so loaded with sensuality, that I'm in no doubt that I've found Senyora Elsa, my Senyora Elsa. Then she, as if she's sensed something, raises her eyes, looks in my direction, and for four seconds—count: one, two, three, four—we stare at each other until, for purely strategic reasons, I close my eyes.

I don't know if she's recognized me. We'll see. Now, with my eyes closed, the music's echoing inside me, going deeper, a single bass sound repeated more and more slowly until it finally stops to envelop me in the darkness of a room in some hotel I'd never heard of before, only two weeks ago, with my best friend, Senyora Elsa's son. And I have memories.

———

Two weeks ago I went to the annual class get-together. Let me say at the outset that this kind of sentimental event annoys me more than anything else. I studied at a private, Catholic, boys-only school run by priests, and over the years my memories of that time—both good and bad— have turned stale and futile, old baggage that does absolutely nothing to help me understand why I am the way I am today. Every year when I come home from the reunion, I have the same feeling, a replay of military service and barracks, which roils unhappily in my entrails, and I tell Tonia, my wife, I'm never going again. But the months go by and, when the date's announced around mid-February, I don't really know why but I hasten to reserve that day in my agenda. I'm aware that this mixture of reluctance and excitement is general and, in fact, people only drop out for really important reasons: heart attack, depression, cancer, prison . . .

The reunion, and I don't mind recognizing it, is guided by a more or less traditional script, maybe because the organizer is Rovirosa, the always-willing, levelheaded friend of everyone, the one who was frequently chosen as class representative and who's now a judge in Madrid. We normally meet on the city outskirts, without wives and kids, midmorning on a Saturday to play a game of soccer. Then we go for lunch in an expensive restaurant on the Maresme coast. We eat fish and shellfish, and liqueurs and cigars draw out the after-dinner conversation. That's when the same old anecdotes are repeated, harmless gripes aired, funny nicknames used, and jokes that seemed hilarious when we were schoolboys retold. Reviving all this is mixed with recent news, which we all handle with care. Sometimes one of the guys knows more than the rest, and disagreeable items can suddenly take on disproportionate importance, as if we all still inhabited the small world of the school. Occasionally there's some loathsome teacher who's died all alone, and we make no effort to hide our pleasure at that. It's a kind of revenge served cold after all the fear and slaps on the head. As the hours go by, we gradually leave, one by one, saying we're very busy, real life calls, and what always happens is that, by the time we get home, the whole comedy is completely forgotten.

If I'm recalling that last alumni meeting now, it's because, two weeks ago, things took quite another turn. Since he was caught up with a complicated trial involving political corruption, Rovirosa couldn't organize it this year, so Boix, who's in the meat trade and an exuberant fellow, suggested a change of scene. Why don't we all go to Cantonigròs? It's only an hour and a half from Barcelona. He knew a very good restaurant where we'd be treated like congressmen. Either because we didn't want to complicate matters, or out of mere inertia, the fact is that no one objected, and on the Saturday in question we all met up in Cantonigròs.

We soon saw that things weren't going to go as planned. We had to cancel the soccer match because of the bad weather. The previous day there'd been a downpour, and when we got to the soccer field, which is normally used by some local amateurs, it was so muddy that the ball kept getting bogged. We did a few halfhearted passes near one of the goals, lumbering moves observed by a herd of cows in the adjacent field, but we soon called it a day. Then we went into town looking for a bar where we could have an appetizer till lunchtime. We sat down by a large window overlooking a landscape of forests and gullies, a view that took in all the immensity of the sky and the world (as Vila-Frau, who's keen on poetry, put it), and after a while, as if watching an apocalyptic diorama, we were treated to one of nature's shows: furious waves of clouds suddenly went still and the sky was gravid with a storm, turning gray and then a menacing nuclear white in just a few minutes. Ten minutes later we were a bunch of kids gleefully watching an army of snowflakes falling, but after an hour, when we were on our way to the restaurant and everything was covered in snow, we started praising the stability of our big cars and some survival instinct made us check to be sure we had cell phone coverage.

The food was splendid, the cigars and liqueurs bore us away from the real world, and by the time we left the restaurant, all the roads in the region were cut off. A couple of the guys weren't resigned to being snowbound and tried to leave, but ten minutes later they were back, tails between their legs and confirming that it was impossible to get out of town. We called home to say we were fine but had to spend the night there, after which, as if we were all on a spiritual retreat, we went off to find a room in Cantonigròs's best hotel.

Once installed, two per room, and our families reassured, we started thinking about how to while away the hours. Some dozed on the sofas in the lounge and others watched the news on TV. We played cards, read newspapers, and condescendingly poked fun at Boix because he got us into this fix. Someone said, "Now, who on earth would think it was a good idea to have lunch in heartland Catalonia?" Someone else added, "We look like a soccer players' jamboree."

I got to share my room with Ingmar, who for many years, when we still believed in these childish things, was my best friend. Ingmar Miralles, son of Senyora Elsa, was born by chance in Gothenburg, where his father was employed at the Spanish consulate, but when he was very small the family moved to Barcelona. At school we were friends from day one because our names were consecutive in the roll call. We did our projects together, went to the same tennis lessons, and described for each other our first experiences of jerking off. Our parents were acquainted and used to go out to dinner as a foursome. At weekends he sometimes slept over at my place or I at his. Life has many twists and turns, and Ingmar, making the most of his knowledge of Swedish as a mother tongue, now lives in Stockholm and we never see each other. This year, though, the alumni meeting coincided with the fact that he was taking a brief vacation in Barcelona, which meant he could come along. Hence, a couple of weeks ago we caught up on what had been happening in our lives. We showed each other photos of laughing children and attractive wives, bad-mouthed some of our classmates who, with the years, have become ridiculous, and planned a trip together to the Land of the Midnight Sun, which we'll probably never do. We also asked after each other's parents, and that's how I found out that Senyora Elsa had separated from her husband quite recently, just a few months earlier. Actually, he ran off with a thirty-year-old secretary and now dyes his hair, wears white sneakers, and has had to learn how to change the diapers of a baby that cries a lot, and all the other clichés you might care to imagine. Oddly enough, Senyora Elsa got over it quite well and was happier than ever: the separation was rejuvenating, she was playing tennis again, had started a course on feng shui, and went out with her women friends on Sunday afternoons (and, at this point, the name of the pub was recalled: the Peculiar). Sometimes, when she'd seemed a little low, Ingmar and his wife had urged her to start over and get a boyfriend, at which she laughed politely but with an edge of irritation.

As if in the grip of coyness, neither Ingmar nor I said

anything about our teenage adventures until we were up in our room, about to go to sleep. After watching TV for a while—channel surfing got us a porn channel and we joked about the Scandinavian actresses—we said good night and turned off the light. But the darkness must have been cozy enough for us to start reliving old times, those long-gone Saturday nights at the Peculiar. We fished in our memories for names and nicknames, the girls with whom we'd both writhed on dusty sofas, sometimes only a week apart. We worked through our old wish lists in some detail and, tittering away, got back to the tennis coach who looked like Farrah Fawcett. She wore little white panties, which, we thought, had to be sweaty: they got scrunched between her buttocks and revealed the most fabulous backside. We deliberately hit the balls into the net so she'd squat down to pick them up, and a few hours later we summoned up the image for our private pleasure.

Now that I think about it, that hotel room in Cantonigròs resembled the setting of our adolescent exchanges of confidences—two beds in the dark—so we both felt displaced, as if we shouldn't be there. In our sniggering, which was perhaps exaggerated, there was a nervous attempt at feeling at ease, at getting around the absurdity of the weekend, and I'm sure that, reliving those nights, we managed to move into another place, another time. Maybe that's why, when we stopped talking and I closed my eyes, instead of going to sleep, I saw, there in the dark of the darkness, the figure of Senyora Elsa taking shape, as if in one of those Magic Eye pictures that were fashionable in those days, and she took me back to a long-ago weekend and the night that she and I sealed our pact in silence.

So there we were, fifteen years old. Franco had died of old age. The cinemas were starting to show movies with actresses who stripped off at the drop of a hat, but we were still minors, so we couldn't get in. Ágata Lys, Nadiuska, Susana Estrada—we knew their names because we saw them seminaked in the magazines we leafed through in the barber's or at newsstands. Sometimes Ingmar slept over at my place on Saturday nights. With the light turned off, talking very quietly so my parents wouldn't hear, we'd get horny telling each other what we liked best about the actresses and then we jerked off in the dark. We said: Nadiuska's got slutty eyes. We said: Victoria Vera's always asking for it, you can see. We'd never seen real live breasts—those of our respective mothers didn't count—let alone pubes. We fooled around with a revolutionary idea. We'd buy some X-Ray Specs by mail order and then go out and look at the underwear of all the girls in the street. We discovered that our fathers had smutty magazines hidden away and when they weren't around we'd get them out, copy the photos of naked girls as accurately as we could, and then exchange them. We said: I want to marry a nympho. We'd never seen any picture of a woman with a shaved pubis, but one day, at Ingmar's place, we found a Swedish magazine in his father's office and there we discovered two things that impressed us even more because they were so daring: a white girl being sodomized by a black guy and, on another page, the compact whiteness of cum splattered on her breasts. We imagined that our tennis coach led a double life and made porn movies with a monitor at the club. We read movie synopses outside cinemas, a lot of them disguising eroticism with histrionic stories of older women falling in love with young gardeners, or gullible foreign girls coming for a holiday by the sea and meekly submitting to the desires of an unscrupulous man. They were so unreal, even for us, that we were both amused and disconcerted. We said "virginity" and "deflower," and the word "perversion" turned us on but we didn't know why.

As I say, we were fifteen and we thought we knew everything about sex, that we were theoretical experts waiting for the practical exam. Then one Saturday night when I slept over at Ingmar's place, I discovered that things weren't quite like that. Locked in his room, we'd been amusing ourselves with the usual fantasies until we got sleepy. After we'd been asleep for about an hour I woke up with a dry mouth and went to get a drink of water. I wandered round the house half-asleep until I found the kitchen, opened the fridge, and instead of water I took a swig of Coca-Cola, straight from the bottle, because no one was watching. Luckily the cold drink must have woken me up—luckily—because when I was going back to the bedroom, past the living room door, I noticed that a floor lamp was switched on and so was the television. I was disoriented and didn't know what time it was, so I peeped round the door expecting to find Ingmar's mother watching TV. Her husband was away on some business trip and my simple imagination figured that she was lonely and sad. I'd say good night, like the well-mannered boy I was. What I saw, though, left me paralyzed and mute. Monotonous drifts of snow shimmied again and again across the TV screen, casting their flickering light over the figure of Senyora Elsa, who'd dropped off to sleep on the sofa.

She lay with a cushion under her head and her skirt rucked up around her waist, showing long, long legs. On tiptoe, without making a sound, I went over to the other end of the sofa to see her better. If she suddenly woke up, I could pretend I was looking for something, a comic book, or whatever else I invented. I stood still, looking at her from above, lying there. Her tousled blond hair fell across her face, and with her eyes closed she looked like one of the actresses we worshipped. Beneath the white blouse her breasts rose and fell in time with her slow breathing.

Having recovered from the first shock, I realized that there on the floor, next to the sofa, lay the tights she'd taken off and, next to them, a scrap of white cloth that could only be panties. I had to smother a squeal of shock. My first instinct was to go and get Ingmar to come and see this, but I immediately realized that it wasn't a good idea. I bent over a little and reverently gazed at that liberated pubis, the first I'd ever seen: the triangular shape; pale, crinkly hairs; thick, plushy fuzz in the center . . . I was dying to touch it, sink my hand into it, but I stayed where I was, unable to move, holding my breath . . . and then, as if she'd sensed my desires, the sleeping Senyora Elsa moved slightly, opening her legs a little more, revealing fleshy red labia. I started panicking, thought she was going to wake up, but the sight of her held me like a magnet. I was rooted to the spot. Suddenly—I don't know whether it was induced by the thick jizz that now smeared my pajama pants—but I thought I saw a kind of tremor, almost imperceptible, shivering through Senyora Elsa's body.

Scared, I took a step, two steps back, seeking the protection of darkness. The rug muffled the movement. If I left, she'd hear me and would almost certainly wake up. In any event, the sight before me had me too transfixed to think about anything else. It wasn't even half a minute before Senyora Elsa moved again on the sofa, and just when I was certain she was going to get up and see me, just when I was busy finding an excuse, I was astounded to see that, no, this wasn't going to happen. With leisurely movements, one of her hands was unbuttoning her blouse, seeking the breasts inside, caressing them, and making the nipples emerge, just poking out from her bra. Meanwhile the other hand had traveled down to her pubis, found the clit, and started rubbing it in rhythmic waves. Now this was field-work! I, that fifteen-year-old boy, understood that Senyora Elsa was pleasuring herself. A few minutes went by and her features were changing into a composition of all the faces of enjoyment, but at no point did she open her eyes. And finally, pressing her lips tightly together, she suppressed a long howl of fulfillment that only I could hear. There in the shadow, an eternity after I'd come without even touching myself, one more surprise awaited me. Senyora Elsa opened her jewel-bright eyes and glanced very briefly at my corner. Then, as if she hadn't seen me, she stood up, pulled down her skirt, picked up her underclothes, turned off the floor lamp and television, and went off to bed, prolonging forever more the mystery that united us.

Now, from other protective shadows in the pub, I realize that, when all is said and done, I know next to nothing about Senyora Elsa except for a few vague biographical details her son told me. Quiet in my past, her presence is empty inside, her personality escapes me, and the fact that I still think about her in that teenage way only shows that I'm fooling myself, because I'm seeing her without the burdens of life that, like everyone else, she's accumulated over the years. The suffering, joys, hopes, and letdowns of aging: everything that has made her who she is, everything that has fledged her existence.

Yet, I don't want my naïveté to be understood as an extenuating circumstance, because in any case I don't believe that my escapade this Sunday is cheating on my wife. No, I'm never going to tell her. It would be doing us no favor and, moreover, it's as if all this stuff isn't really happening . . . So many negative formulations. Maybe all this is upending my sense of reality, and accepting that every decision I've made so far to the point of coming here, to the Peculiar, comes from this Sunday morning; but, then again, maybe it's been growing inside me—like a chrysalis that refuses to leave the cocoon —for a good part of my life.

I love sleeping in, and I suppose the busy hands of my daughter, Roser, aged three and a half, had been trying to get me to open my eyes for a while before I finally woke up. From behind my eyelids, still half-asleep, I could hear my wife wishing me "Good morning" in a singsong cartoon-movie voice, and Roser's voice repeating it in the same tone. Smiling, I pretended to keep sleeping, waiting for her to make me open my eyes again. When she did, I suddenly sat up and started tickling her. Roser expected this and, somehow, played her part in all innocence, because recently this is her favorite game: getting into bed with us early in the morning, between the two of us, and fooling around till we wake up and play with her.

Today, after the tickling attack, we made a tent under the comforter and the three of us took refuge in it because there was a raging storm outside and we had to seek protection together. I puffed and swooshed, imitating the sound of wind and rain, but Roser suddenly went quiet. She was frightened because it was difficult for her to understand that we were only playing. Then Tonia lifted up the comforter in time—"Hey, we're fine!"—when Roser was already screwing up her face to cry, and I grabbed her and hoisted her up with my feet so she could be an airplane, which I know she likes, and her loud, clear, contagious giggles rang out again. A few seconds later some movement of hers—silky feet caressing my back (I don't use pajamas) or her arms hugging my thigh—aroused some nerve I didn't know about and brought on an instant erection. I realized what had happened, of course, and looked at Tonia, wordlessly asking her to distract Roser while I covered the inappropriate festival with a pillow trying to make it subside.

"*It's all OK, I say OK,*" I sang pretending everything was fine. "*It's just me, just physiology.*"

"It's all OK, as you say," Tonia repeated soothingly, *"except that you men are a bunch of animals. What a waste . . ."*

Then she took Roser off to the kitchen to get breakfast together, but the mists of resentment hung over the bedroom. I know where all this is coming from, but it needs some explanation. About six months ago, Tonia told me she wanted another baby, a son. In the past, before Roser was born, we'd agreed that one was enough, so at first I tried to talk her out of it. Roser's keeping us busy and entertained enough, I argued and, even if money's not a problem, another kid would mean losing a bit more of that freedom we cherished so much when there were just the two of us. Had she forgotten? All those trips, holidays, dinners, and movies. Maybe it was just physiology again, but, no, she didn't get my reasoning at all. She thought I was being selfish and even mean, so I gave in. All right, then, let's try for another one. Everyone says the second kid is easier, I tried to convince myself, rationalizing that, when the time came, I'd even be happy about it. But the months went by, the periods came, and there was no sign of a pregnancy. With all the pressures of hitting the bull's-eye, sex was getting more mechanical, more predictable, more boring. We no longer fucked when we felt like it but on the days decreed by the fertility calendar, and our postcoital pillow talk turned into an ongoing biology lesson. Tonia joined a yoga class for women who were trying to conceive, and I was finding it more and more difficult to get a hard-on. One failure was the prelude to another, a mental state in withdrawal, everyday love turned into a retractile appendage. That's why, when Tonia saw the glory of my useless erection this morning, she confirmed yet again that the world is unfair and held me responsible by default. The psychologists call it passive aggression.

And here comes part two of the difficult situation that has led me to the Peculiar. When breakfast was ready, Tonia called me and I went to the kitchen. As usual, Roser's happy little presence calmed us down. Croissants, still warm from the oven, swaddled us in that Sunday morning fragrance, and we did justice in silence to the perfect family scene. Then Roser sat on my lap—no mishap, don't worry—and Tonia even made some flippant comment about my rampant libido. We laughed again. Flipping through the Sunday magazine, I spotted an interview with a Rolling Stones guitarist who, about to turn seventy, had recently married a girl who could be his daughter or granddaughter and they had a baby. The story reminded me of Ingmar's father and his new life as a granddaddy-daddy, and I told Tonia because I thought it would move things out of our own terrain. The old tactic of projecting your shit onto someone famous. Error.

"You see?" Her tone had a ring of sarcasm, which is something new. "You men are all the same. Physiology, as you say. You see some young girl and you can only think with your dick. It's revolting." She went quiet for a few seconds, pensive as she flicked through the magazine, perhaps waiting for me to answer, but I was careful not to open my mouth and only nodded. Then she added, "Please don't ever do that to me. If you're going to cheat on me someday, please let it be with an older woman and not with a twenty-year-old who knows nothing about life. I can't think of anything more mortifying. Imagine what it was like for that woman, the mother of your Swedish friend. What a drama."

I said I couldn't agree more, gave her a conciliatory kiss, and changed the subject, but her words kept floating in my brain, instantly linking up with Ingmar's words two weeks earlier, his amused account of Senyora Elsa's new life, her Sundays at the pub, and I put it all together to conclude that I had to find her and the sooner the better. Sometimes you have to take a step backwards in order to advance two ahead. Maybe it was callow, but somehow the solution to the problem involved making me feel like a teenager again, as pure as I was at the age of fifteen, let's say. Then I got it. It was so obvious. The soccer match in a bar with friends was the perfect excuse.

I went to take a shower. At this point, inspired by my faith in the turn of events, I could pretend that I closed my eyes to keep the soap out, and when I opened them I was in the pub, leaning on the bar and flirting at a distance with Senyora Elsa, my best friend's mother . . .

So I open my eyes again in the Peculiar and see that Senyora Elsa has sat down again with her friends. The lingering look we exchanged a moment ago contained all the information necessary, the coded message both of us are looking for this Sunday afternoon, and I'm certain she knows how to interpret it. I see a waiter going over to her table with another bowl of peanuts and to ask if they want anything else. Then, with an awkward movement of his arm, he knocks over Senyora Elsa's drink of whatever-and-whatever. There's a clatter of glass, the ladies cry out in surprise, and she stands up in the middle of the group to inspect her wet skirt. The waiter apologizes and she tells him not to worry, but then she says goodbye to her friends. She comes toward the bar and, walking past without looking at me, tells the waiter in a confidential tone that she's going home to change and she'll be back shortly. I give her a lead of a few meters, pay for my drink, and also leave.

Outside, it's already dark, I'm disoriented, and at first I don't know which direction she's taken, but finally I see her. I move a little faster until I'm about thirty paces behind her. We walk along Passeig de la Bonanova for a while, its sidewalks now reviving in my memory. I know we're going to cross Ganduxer, and when we get to the corner with Escoles Pies, we'll turn left and go downhill. Now she turns and I lose sight of her, but I'm not worried, because I know that her place, Ingmar's place, is the fifth or sixth door along that sidewalk. I also turn and walk down the street. I see her stop, open the door, and go inside. For a moment I expect a knowing look from her, some recognition of the situation that will tell me I'm on the right track. But no. As I go over, I try to recall which apartment she lived in—lives in—because I've made up my mind to ring the bell, but when I get to the street door I see she's left it ajar. Desire tells me it's an invitation to go up, but in any case I look at the mailboxes to check which apartment it is (and see her Swedish surname beneath the name Miralles, which has a black line drawn through it) and then go out again and ring her doorbell. She opens without saying a word. Now there's no doubt. I go up in the elevator, knowing that when I reach her landing, I'll find her door slightly open, that I'll slowly go inside without making a sound and, with the shyness of a young boy, I'll look for the living room.

Meanwhile Senyora Elsa has taken off her stained dress and is lying on the sofa. When I go in, I see that everything is the same as it used to be, twenty years ago. The rug, the floor lamp, the TV. I go over to her and see that she's looking me up and down and smiling. I'm slightly unnerved by this very candid reception but understand it's part of the game. Her breasts are heaving inside her bra, the nipples standing up, chafing to escape. I see that she's wearing black tights today with white panties underneath. They instantly turn me crazy. As if making up for my timidity that first time, I go over to her, kneel by her side, and do what I didn't do then. I put my hand inside her panties and plunge it between her thighs. She gasps and her hand comes looking for me. She undoes my zip—I'm on fire—and fondles my cock. I take off my shoes, socks, and trousers and climb onto the sofa so we're in sixty-nine position. Things happen, but I won't go into detail, because I'm not fifteen anymore. I realize that I so badly wanted this to happen, that I needed it so much, that I could be here many Sunday afternoons until I grow up again and yet still miss her in the same primitive, calculated way as I did this morning. She, however, looks me in the eyes for the first time, asks my name, and tells me to get my clothes off.

So all the clothes are flung off and I'm riveted by her

bronzed tennis player's body as if she's still that young mother. (I shake my head to get rid of the image of my wife, Tonia, who, from home, rebukes me for the thought.) She's my best friend's mother, I tell myself, and now, with dazzling insight, I understand that the debauchery I saw in her as an adolescent, the apparent wantonness, was actually unique sexual honesty, a liberation that came from the north of Europe and, in that uptight Barcelona, in that well-heeled part of town, must have been extremely rare. Despite everything, her free, sexy spontaneity has come through the years as a secret, all the way to the present, reached today, reached here in this feast of two strangers. Now I'm the one lying on the sofa letting her have her way with me. She's in charge, she's Senyora Elsa, and I swear I feel like a kid who has everything to learn. We're entangled wordlessly, using only the language of moans. After a while we know we're close to the climax, our bodies are plummeting, spinning, and she lets out a cry from the depths of her soul, a joyful groan, and collapses on top of me. I've grown up very fast. Then Senyora Elsa opens her eyes and, looking at me so tenderly it almost hurts, asks, "What did you say your name is?"

SEVEN DAYS
ON THE LOVE BOAT

If life had treated him well, he might have been one of those capricious billionaires with a mansion on the French Riviera or the Adriatic coast: a cute palace surrounded by gardens where he'd collect crazy things like a swimming pool shaped like a grand piano, a huge bed shaped like a grand piano, and—in the most select part of the living room, next to a picture window presenting the sea as a continuation of the cliff top—a perfectly tuned grand piano in see-through glass showing off its intimate workings of strings and keys.

If life had treated him well. But, in fact, it didn't treat him well enough, at least until the day I said goodbye to him forever and left behind a slow, unsteady week, always about to be wrecked in a labyrinth of too-narrow passageways, obliging barmen and cabin stewards, karaoke championships, and cocktails at unearthly hours.

I met Sam Cortina, alias "Tap Dance Fingers," alias "Velvet Voice," during a Mediterranean cruise. It was May, a May so shaken up by climate change that the weathermen were salivating at the mere prospect of the historic heat wave records that were soon to be broken. Bet and I had been married seven years. In order to celebrate this—and without telling her—I'd booked us a week in Paris, in a spectacular hotel recommended in a Sunday magazine. It was supposed to be a surprise, even a deliberately schmaltzy surprise, as these lovefests often tend to be; but a few days beforehand, one Saturday afternoon, she freaked out over something, and all hell broke loose. We fought for three hours, going round and round the same old recriminations, and then out they came, the fatal words—"Let's take a break, Mauri, at least for a couple of weeks, and then we'll see what happens"—setting my future alight and, with that, those days in Paris, which became a prematurely carbonized memory. The passage of time burns memories, too, first turning them into dry parchment, after which the combustion starts at the corners, but at least it grants us the illusion of experience.

The fact is that things between us hadn't been good for a while. We squabbled over all kinds of stupid issues and had built a castle of mutual rancor too weighty and too hard for us to bear, but I saw the trip to Paris as a chance to fix things, like those peace talks between enemy countries that are held on neutral ground. We didn't make it in time. It must be said, though, that for the first time our argument took a civilized course without shouting, slamming doors, or crying, and maybe that's why I didn't dare to mention our little trip at any point or wave it in front of her face as a token of love she'd unwittingly ruined.

Although it was a civilized temporary separation, I got mad after a couple of days. I know myself, and there was no way it wasn't going to happen. That Saturday night we agreed that I'd sleep on the sofa bed in the guest room. The next day, just as it was getting light, she woke me up with a friendly, almost conciliatory smile (and swollen eyes after all the crying) to tell me she was going to stay with one of her friends and would call me in a few days. I watched her leave with a suitcase and a duffel bag ridiculously stuffed full of clothes and books as if she were going to the ends of the earth. I heard her close the door, and, now fully awake, the only thing I could do was to run my eyes over the walls of the guest room. That impersonal decoration of chipped vases, faded cushions, and framed posters we'd got tired of looking at in the dining room, and those shelves lined with old college books no longer said anything about us. I felt like a total schmuck.

Sunday went by swathed in mindless calm like a toothache relieved by a painkiller. I didn't go out all day, didn't even change out of my pajamas, and, as well as a schmuck, I felt like a useless imbecile. So I started hating my wife. Looking back, now that everything has changed, I can see that the word is too strong. It's not too difficult to understand that, if this really was the case, I hated her as a simple defense mechanism, so as not to hate myself even more.

On Monday the hatred started taking shape. By then I was operating in a primal, instinctive mode and had made no real effort to work out what it was that had led us to this temporary separation. When I tried to think it through, the frustrated trip to Paris—sure, without her even knowing about it—took up the whole scene and blinded me to anything else. As soon as I could, that morning I called work and told the secretary I wouldn't be coming in, as I was ill. I don't think it was a lie. Then I showered, made some coffee, and went to the travel agency. Since the week in Paris was already paid for and had cost a small fortune, I decided to reinvest all the money *against* my wife, which is to say to extract some kind of sexual yield from it.

I admit that I was probably being an idiot reacting like that, but now, with the perspective of some months, I see it as a kind of forward regress. And this might sound cynical, but I was doing it out of fidelity. I told the guy at the travel agency that we couldn't go to Paris because Bet had an inescapable work commitment. "Basically we're twenty-first-century slaves," he confirmed. I also told him that I had to take my holidays then because I was exhausted. Since I hadn't stinted and money was no problem, I'd thought about a trip to some distant exotic place like Thailand or Vietnam. The travel agency guy immediately understood what I was looking for. Moving closer to gain my trust, he told me that this was impossible because of the limited time, and I had to understand that you can't do anything in a week. Then he started telling me about a Mediterranean cruise, the excellent weather forecasts for those dates, and all the people who, after the dreariness of winter, wanted a high-seas experience to take it easy and have some fun. "It's another world," he said and, confidently driving home his point, added, "You'll like it."

Hence, on our seventh wedding anniversary, instead of celebrating it with Bet over dinner in a restaurant in Paris, with soft candlelight and jazz playing in the background, I was wandering around like a soul in torment through the passageways of a transatlantic liner with a ridiculous name, *Wonderful Sirena*, with smoked salmon and Roquefort ravioli clumping in my stomach and about to hear the voice and piano of Sam Cortina for the first time.

The *Wonderful Sirena* was a hulking great thing sailing under an Italian flag and with pretensions of being a floating metropolis. The travel agency's information leaflets said it could accommodate as many as twelve hundred passengers in its cabins, but I never saw it full in the week I spent on board. Its route through part of the Mediterranean traced a circle, and passengers boarded and disembarked in every port. The day I embarked, the ship was sailing for Alicante, and from there to Tunis, Valletta in Malta, Sicily, Naples, Marseille, and back to Barcelona. If you followed the itinerary on a map, tracing it out with little red lines, it was as if the sea were an immense blue canvas, a circus tent, and the ship was stitching it up at every port. We, of course, were there inside: toothless lions, ancient elephants, and mournful seals.

When we docked in any port, always before midday,

the passengers had almost a whole day to disembark, get on a bus, tour the city, and buy souvenirs in shops indicated by a local guide. Then, when everyone was back on board again, now joined by new passengers, the ship put out to sea once more—at dusk—and the Mediterranean coast disintegrated into thousands of specks of light as we returned to the lunar weightlessness of the night sea.

In the whole week I didn't leave the ship, not even once. I heard the names of cities and was paralyzed by disinclination. Sometimes, lying in bed in my cabin and staring fixedly at the ceiling, it seemed I'd never left the guest room at home. I only cheered up when I went up on deck to look at the profile of the city we'd been to that day with the racket of the port in the foreground and streets climbing away from it. Sometimes I imagined that I was going down to terra firma, diving into one of those narrow winding streets, never to return, but this temptation to start over in another corner of the world was too literary, too fabulous, for someone like me. Now I think that, if I didn't leave the ship to walk around the cities, it was because it wouldn't have made sense without Bet. My years with her had made me realize there's not much pleasure in solitary tourism.

That first day, a Friday afternoon, I boarded the ship an hour before she set sail. Once I got through the reception formalities, a Filipino cabin steward, speaking a mixture of Italian, French, and Spanish and smiling all the while, took my bag and showed me where my cabin was, on deck three, starboard side. As I followed him, I counted five identical passageways, carpeted in cardinal red and lined with dozens of doors. He opened the door of cabin 3014, first class. A square—no, not round—porthole gave a view of the end of the port breakwater and, beyond that, the open sea. *"Buonasera, signor,"* the steward said from the door, and left without waiting for a tip. Alone in the cabin, I unpacked my luggage, hung clothes in the wardrobe to get rid of creases, and lay down on the double bed, waiting impatiently for the boat to leave, finally leave. I closed my eyes, imagining that on the other side of the door an erotic festival in my honor was being rehearsed, a parade of lovely, accessible, voluptuous women winding through the passageways. And they'd be available after midnight, as if by paying for my ticket I'd been guaranteed that one or another of them would make my dream come true.

It was pure fantasy, of course. I must have dropped off to sleep like a little kid tired out after all the turmoil, but then I was woken by three long deep blasts of the ship's horn announcing that we were leaving. I looked out the porthole and saw that Barcelona was still just a stone's throw away. With sham nostalgia, I gazed at the two Olympic towers, the tidy containers in the cargo port, the bulk of Montjuïc. Until it all dissolved into night. Now I know: traveling round the Mediterranean on a cruise ship instills in the passengers a liking for staring at the horizon, which is often artificial.

But never mind. I don't want to get sidetracked by that. The point is that I was unable to leave my cabin that night. I'd woken up feeling drained and semicomatose, immediately aware that no one on the ship was going to miss me.

More than once, hearing footsteps and cheerful voices in the passageway, I feared someone would knock at the door and try to come in. All night long I tossed and turned in a shallow, clammy sleep, as if I were in a bathtub full of lukewarm water and had to be careful to get my head up every minute to breathe.

Luckily, the next day swept away all those fears, and I got up in a different mood. It was Saturday, the sun was shining, and I had a mission. While having breakfast in an on-deck café, I studied and learned by heart the ship's list of activities. Among other attractions, leisure-time amusements on the *Wonderful Sirena* included three nightclubs, two theaters, and two swimming pools. Keen golfers could improve their swing during the day by hitting organic balls that turned into fish food once they were in the sea. The word "bored" was banned and "Mediterranean parties" lasting till sunup were organized every night. I read the whole list of pastimes and, with my illusions still intact, looked up and watched the people on deck. They were strolling round, gummy-eyed, slow-moving, ecstatic. The men sported Bermuda shorts in a great array of tartans, and the women smelled like the vaguely Provençal soap provided in the cabins. More than one person carried a book and a cocktail, searching for deck chairs in which to keep dozing, books lying open on bellies. I dismissed a reactionary thought extolling the aristocratic cruises of yore because they would have excluded me, too, and once I'd finished my coffee, I went off to imitate the masses.

Like everyone else, having roamed the deck all morning, I devoted the afternoon to exploring the entrails of the whale. I covered the length of the ship, the six decks from bow to stern, port to starboard, and soon saw that this was no aquatic metropolis but a huge shopping mall. I had to get lost ten times at different levels and in their grid pattern of symmetrical streets to understand the liner's urban planning: general attractions clustered in the middle and cabins gathered around them at both ends.

Since I wanted to socialize, I hung around in the shopping zone. In the luxury boutiques I tried to make eye contact with some of the haughty, ennui-stricken women shoppers who couldn't hold a seductive gaze if it didn't have dollar signs stamped on it. I stopped for a moment outside the beauty center with its wildly gesticulating, obsequious hairdresser, who was probably a failed artist. A sign offered tattoos and piercings for those seeking strong emotions. I went into the gym where a flock of elderly folk were showing off new tracksuits their children had given them for Christmas. Pillboxes tinkled in pockets as they rode the stationary bikes. I wandered among the bustling tables in the miniature casino, which had an exit onto the promenade deck in case some desperate soul wanted to take a dive into the sea after losing everything.

I also had an otherworldly sensation that I should describe. As you moved away from the ship's sparkling center, the light in the passageways became increasingly tenuous, the shadows mistier and fleeting. I'm not talking about paranormal phenomena but just saying it was quite evident that, at the outer edges of the world of brightness, shy passengers traveling alone, centrifuged away and banished from leisure activities, were mooching round these corridors with eyes of a beaten dog. In every corner, near windows looking out, they stopped to check if they had cell phone reception at last.

I suspected they were outcasts and I didn't want to be one of them—not yet—so I went looking for a restaurant where I could have dinner. I chose the self-service, because I figured that trays laden with food, all nicely set out, and the ceremony of getting up and walking around with your plate favored contact with people. To break the ice, you could always say to the person next to you how great the trunk of hake à la Basque looks, or even joke about the glutton who's got up from the table five times to get another serving of paella. I was counting on a predisposition to good humor, on people wanting to have some fun, but all I got were a few cautiously courteous smiles or, to be more precise, three from women and two (much more open) from men. A friend of mine going back to our high school days, a born optimist, would have called it "building infrastructure." But as I've already suggested, I opted for satiating my disappointment with smoked salmon and Roquefort ravioli, knowing I'd have all night to regret it.

Before bedtime, I went out to pace the deck again, up and down, tenaciously trying to get my dinner moving. At sea, the night was warm and the gentle breeze brought a kind of static electricity that numbed the senses. Under the full moon the deck was like a small-town promenade on a Sunday evening in summer. People nodded at each other. Some faces were starting to look familiar, maybe from the restaurant or the shops, but it wasn't worth trying to speak with anyone. (I mean that they wouldn't have contributed to the point of my journey.) Half a dozen brattish kids were fooling around, splashing each other in the lit-up swimming pool astern. In a couple of deck chairs normally used for sunbathing but now tucked away out of the light, I spotted two women chatting and smoking. Like me, they were over thirty and looked as if they'd been telling all their secrets. When I was cooking up some excuse for approaching them, the loudspeakers announced a spectacular fireworks display, and everyone looked up at the sky waiting for the first rocket. The two women—champagne ad look-alikes, one blond and the other brunette—stood up and went over to the railing. When they walked past me they started whispering and pretended they didn't know I was there, but a few steps further on they burst out laughing. Knotted at the waist, their pareus flew in the breeze.

I miscalculated. I must have gotten carried away with the fireworks, trusting that they'd also be looking at them, but when I tried to find them again after last explosion of light, they'd completely disappeared. An hour later, now after midnight, I'd fruitlessly checked out the three nightclubs. My feet hurt. I was a sad poor wretch and there was no one to console me. Then, luckily, I discovered the piano bar where Sam Cortina played, and no sooner had I walked in, sat at the bar, and asked for a whisky sour than his voice washed over me, balm for my weariness, succor for my anxieties.

The piano bar was called the Rimini. It appeared out of nowhere, hiding behind thick curtains, a clandestine oasis that adopted me like a little orphan for the whole week. The barman wore a tux and a red bow tie. They opened when it got dark and closed—*if* they closed—at sunup. The place was shaped like a number eight, with a circular bar at one end. Around the other circle, dim in russet shadows, you could detect some velvet sofas. A few brand-new couples were making the most of the intimacy they afforded to do a bit of warming up before deciding whose cabin. Those of us sitting at the bar watched them leave, somewhere between envious and hopeful because we, too, were part of the scene. At the other end was Sam Cortina playing the piano. Next to the piano, a stand displayed a faded poster announcing, "With you today, Sam Cortina, Tap Dance Fingers, three years undisputed king in Caesars Palace, Las Vegas." Occasionally someone, maybe Sam himself, turned the poster around so that it read, in a more classical design, "With you today, Sam Cortina, Velvet Voice, king of Atlantic City." After a couple of nights, I understood that "today" meant always, eternally.

I recall that when I walked into the piano bar, Sam Cortina was playing a Neil Diamond song, "Solitary Man." Since then, I've listened to it over and over again: "But until I can find me / . . . I'll be what I am / A solitary man . . ." Accompanied only by the piano, Sam Cortina sang it slower than Neil Diamond, lingering over every word, massaging out all the feeling. The velvet voice, breaking at the perfect point of a flaw, aging, elegant, rounded out the desolation. Yet the final effect wasn't excessively sad. *That song's about me,* I thought. *It's a coded message.* How gullible, how ingenuous I was. It didn't even take five more songs for me to understand that Sam was singing for himself.

His repertoire was so well chosen he never fell into the trap of routine. He could alternate Cole Porter and Irving Berlin evergreens with Joni Mitchell and James Taylor ballads. He always started with Jobim, something different every day. His signature. He sang Stevie Wonder with echoes of Frank Sinatra. He took on Gainsbourg when it got very late. Physically, he looked like Burt Bacharach if he sang his songs, and there was no need for choirs or violins. He knew how to choose what he did of the Beatles.

And speaking of the Beatles, that first night when I beached up in the piano bar, just when I was finishing my third whisky sour and the barman was making me another one at his own initiative, Sam Cortina started to play "Yesterday." I always cry when I hear "Yesterday." I can't and don't want to avoid it. The first three notes are enough to trigger some deep wellspring that fills my eyes with tears. I've never been to see any specialist. I'm cool about it. It's a song that cracks me up in a millisecond. It can come from Muzak in a department store, watered down in Fausto Papetti's version, in Marvin Gaye's more emotional rendering, reconstructed by Miles Davis's trumpet, or even warped into a lullaby. My wife, Bet, thinks it's funny, because, according to her, I've chosen the corniest song in the world to get soppy over. Sometimes at home she hums it in my ear to surprise me. It could be to make fun of me, pretending that she's crying, too, or because—and now I see it—it actually really moves her.

When Sam Cortina played it that night, with a long piano introduction before he started singing, I whimpered with feeling I'd never known before, a more genuine feeling, I'd say, as if all the liters of tears I'd shed in my life until then were just a rehearsal for this one occasion. I sang it softly to myself and I'm sure I was babbling.

I mopped up my tears with a paper napkin. The barman gave me a supportive smile. Only a few stalwarts were left in the Rimini: two couples marooned on their sofas, a British husband and wife being bored together, and three sojourners like myself leaning on the bar. When he finished "Yesterday," Sam Cortina thanked his audience and announced a break. There were a few attempts at lazy, desultory applause. I was the only one who clapped loud and long. He came down from the stage and sat beside me. The waiter brought him a whisky, no ice.

"Men don't cry," he said after taking a sip of his drink, and winked at me. I gave back what I suppose was a bovine stare and blinked to see him better. He was tall, skinny, but broad-shouldered. His hair was whitish-gray and well cut. His skin bronzed and dry. I thought he was about sixty. He had class, the class of a displaced pianist. I'm not saying he had airs, but he was definitely too classy for that piano bar on the *Wonderful Sirena*.

"'Yesterday' has been a weakness of mine for years," I said, "and you stirred it up again. I imagine I should be grateful. Your whisky's on me."

I wobbled slightly on my stool but, hearing my voice, I realized I wasn't as drunk as I thought.

"Here my whisky's always on the house. This is my place." He tilted his glass in a sort of toast, long, thin fingers cradling the drink with languor acquired over years. We spoke English, and his American accent was still tinged with lees of the Italian his parents had spoken. At first sight and from the outside, Sam Cortina seemed to be living on the fringes of human passions. The conversation that night and those that were to follow in the next few days were to confirm this first impression. Sam presented himself in public as nerveless, poised, the guy who's seen it all, and his coolness—on board a cruiser and transmitted to the audience—gave him an aura of inscrutability which protected him like armor plating.

I asked him about Las Vegas and Atlantic City, and he described the outlandish glamor of the big casinos where you never know whether it's day or night, the tedium of playing with an orchestra that only does medleys of the big hits, a dozen shows a week. Without making a big deal of it, he mentioned in passing that he'd played with José Feliciano, Barry Manilow, and Liza Minnelli. He reminisced about those old times without a trace of emotionality, and it was only when we went back to the subject of music, the carefully chosen songs of his repertoire, that his expression recovered the verve he'd shown onstage. Nonetheless, he took advantage of a lull in the conversation to change the subject.

"Forgive me for returning to your tears before, but there's a woman behind that, isn't there?"

"There's always a woman. You'd know better than anyone. All those songs you played tonight talk about the same thing."

He gestured in false modesty, in slight rebuttal.

"I asked because it's not the first or the second time I've seen this happen. Men cry more often than people imagine. They have to be alone, yes, sure. They need to atone for something. Are you traveling alone?"

"Look, I'll be honest with you: I boarded yesterday afternoon with the intention of having an affair and cheating on my wife. But, for the moment, the whole thing's a dead loss. Right now, if I could, I think I'd jump in a lifeboat and row back home."

"Ah, now I get it. So basically you were crying with rage."

"Dunno," I muttered. The whisky sour was pumping through my blood. My tongue felt thick and gluey. It might have been a warning to stop the conversation right there, but I didn't pick it up.

"Be patient. Don't play the victim and it'll all be fine. I've been working on this boat eight years now and I think I know what you need. There's one detail that doesn't appear in the cruise brochures and it's very important. Listen to me: the best thing to do is to go looking among the crew members. Flings between passengers never end well because everyone expects too much, and the goodbyes are too sudden, leaving everyone unsatisfied. By contrast, when it all ends, the crew stays on board, if you get what I mean."

"Perfectly."

"You can pay, of course—you've got the whole kit and caboodle here—but, for that, you don't need to get on a boat." He paused and, turning slightly in the direction of the sofas, lowered his voice. "Over there in the corner, for example, you have those two who've just got together. I don't know where he came on board. Maybe Marseille. She's Italian, from Naples, and she's been working as a waitress in the pizzeria for the last six months. She's very homesick, they tell me, and when she finishes her shift, the only thing she does is walk around the deck, staring at the horizon in the direction of Italy. Someone always approaches her and they start talking. Then two and two are four."

"Two and two are four," I parroted.

"Nobody in this world wants to be alone. The tourist coordinators, waitresses, receptionists, salesclerks, cooks, beauticians . . . If you're not too fussy, you'll get what you want."

"And for you, meanwhile, the elegant rich ladies in first class. I get your drift . . . ," I said.

He laughed with his eyes, a silent snicker, and pushed his glass over to the barman for a refill.

"I'm not in the game anymore," he said. "I won't deny that in the early years it was a pushover. I've known ladies from around the world and, if you'll forgive my boasting, couldn't count how many different languages I've made love in, but now I'm retired." He said these words still clinging to a certain vanity, but then, after a pause to take a sip of his whisky, he added, "I'm a loser. Don't be fooled by me."

In fact, the words tumbled out of him. His face changed for a second, as if he were plunging into an abyss, but then he realized what was happening and looked me in the eye with the same firmness as before, adopting a haughty air. He quickly started talking again in order to circumvent any comment I might make.

"You look like a smoker and I'd really like a cigarette, but smoking's banned in here because they say we'll set fire to the carpet. Follies of modern times. By way of compensation, though, they let us take our drinks out on the deck. Want to come?"

There was hardly anyone on deck. The full moon swept the calm sea, shining on us like a spotlight on a stage. We smoked in silence, each absorbed in his own world. Then Sam announced he was going back to the piano bar. He still had to play another hour for nobody. I decided to go to bed and we introduced ourselves as we said good night. Sam. Mauri. Shaking his hand, I said, "There's something I've been wanting to ask you, Sam. Where do you live? Where's your home?"

He was silent for a couple of seconds. "Here," he said. "I live here. On the ship."

———

I don't think it'll be a spoiler if I reveal at this point in the story that my wife and I are back together again. Not long ago we celebrated our eighth anniversary—in Paris—two weeks after the actual date, because we decided not to count on our calendar the fortnight we were separated. I guess it's not a spoiler, as I say, because at the heart of this story I'm not talking about her but about Sam Cortina. My wife still doesn't know who he is. I've never mentioned him, but at some level she senses he's there. Sometimes, when we're arguing again, she'll drop a hint, saying I was different when I came back home, but she never goes further than that because she knows this territory's out of bounds. In our tacit reconciliation agreements, I gave in to some things she thought were important and she had to accept my silence, which sometimes—I admit it—can be as mysterious as a dolphin's smile.

After that first conversation with Sam Cortina, I spent the next three days stuck in what we might call the routine of disappointment. Day in day out, the *Wonderful Sirena* docked in some port in the morning, people disembarked to have some fun, and we set sail again at dusk. In the afternoons she was semideserted and, taking Sam's advice, I tried my luck with the female crew members. No go. I learned to forget about the Filipinas who worked in the laundry doing the washing and ironing and, in general, all the Asian women, because they only giggled and avoided me, pretending they didn't understand anything. The Italian cooks and waitresses played along for a while but never let it go any further. A twenty-two-year-old Frenchwoman gave me a manicure and pedicure. Her soft, warm hands tidied up cuticles and filed my nails with promising intimacy, but she avoided my gaze the whole time. And Sam, who knew her from having his nails done, had assured me that she's not shy. Since I didn't want to get a bad name on the ship, after day four, I was much more selective in my attempts at seduction and sought chance encounters in the narrow passageways. And that only gave me the sensation of being an outcast. Sometimes I found a quiet corner with cell phone coverage and listened to my voicemail. Bet was phoning every day, and every day her voice sounded more concerned and understanding. It was mainly this detail that spurred me on in my mission.

When darkness fell, routine led me to the Rimini. I only had to walk in for the barman to start making my whisky sour and Sam to greet me from the piano, just raising his eyebrows and not looking at me. The British couple soldiered on with their project of getting through the whole cocktail list. If I spotted one of my day's endeavors clasped in other arms, my pride took a blow. I bet with the guys at the bar on how long it would take before they headed off to one of the cabins. We also informed each other, with a spot of melancholy, about people who'd definitely left the boat. At some point Sam always played the opening notes of "Yesterday," as if about to launch into a long overture, and then, when tears started pricking my eyes, he changed course and sang a completely different song.

If I'd taken the time to write a ship's log, it would note that on the Tuesday, my fifth day on board, there were major changes. That morning the sky was dingy, with low clouds, and the light coming through my cabin porthole wasn't as bright as it had been on other days. I woke up in a state of revived affective alertness. The previous night we'd left Naples behind and, as you might say, we were on the home run. My chances were dwindling. During my midday walk, attracted by a clamor of voices, I went into a ballroom, which I'd never entered before, and discovered one of the two women—the brunette—I'd semipursued the night of the fireworks. I watched her for quite a while and then deferentially approached. She was sitting at a table, jotting down a whole lot of names in a notebook. I asked her what she was doing and she said she was a presenter and was preparing for the karaoke duets championship, an activity designed so people could meet. She spoke a very amorous-sounding mixture of Italian and Spanish, and her voice was so persuasive that a minute later I was looking for my partner in the competition.

I found Anja from Sweden and, yes, she was my shipboard lady. I never asked how old she was but I imagine around forty-five. She was blond, married, a mother—doing the trip with her sister Marianne—very Scandinavian, and I'll sum up her appeal and romantic disposition with the image of a black thong under white Bermuda shorts. Yes, on the prowl. In the karaoke duets championship, Anja and I did a song called "Guilty," which Barbra Streisand and Barry Gibb (the Bee Gees guy) made famous. If you know it, you'll also know that it's a very difficult song, especially the bits where his falsetto comes in. The presenter handed us a copy of the lyrics and we rehearsed a few times, hidden away in a discreet corner of the deck. We were laughing a lot. If Sam had heard us singing, he would have stopped speaking to me. Finally, because of the question of high and low notes, we decided that I'd be Barbra and Anja would be Barry, and this formal pirouette worked very nicely for us, to the point of our coming second in the championship. A pair of Belgians who sang "Ain't No Mountain High Enough" by Marvin Gaye and Tammi Terrell were the winners. They nailed it.

Anja pronounced my name French-style, "Moguí" instead of "Mauri." Onstage, we learned to hold hands and gaze deeply into each other's eyes as we sang falsetto, "We got nothing to be sorry for / Our love . . . is one in a million . . ." And it was true, we didn't have to apologize for anything because our love—or whatever it was that united us right then and there—was one in a million. We didn't have to feel guilty, as the title of the song suggested. A shipboard photographer, one of those guys who always want to capture your moments of happiness and sell them back to you at exorbitant prices, took our picture in the final round. If I look at it now—because I still have it—I think we were acting and that's all. But I also relive, with a touch of nostalgia, the calm that suffused me when at last life swept me up and I knew my place on the cruise ship, the role that was mine to play in the cast of the floating opera.

That night we were invited to the official black-tie dinner. The winning Belgian couple, Anja, and I were seated at the captain's table. At dessert time we were handed the runners-up cup for the karaoke duets championship. (Applause. Another photo.) It was silver plated and, hastily engraved on the front, were our misspelled names, Anya and Maury, the errors making the whole thing even more fabulous. We filled it with champagne, made a toast, and drank out of it together, our mouths very close. People came over to the table to congratulate us, calling us Barry and Barbra. The sparkle was with us all night. Anja and her sister had boarded in Naples, one day earlier, and their pleasure tanks were overflowing. They were unstoppable. First, the three of us, and then Anja and I alone—because Marianne gave us the slip and disappeared—drank exotic cocktails in a bar that imitated a bamboo hut, and then we went to dance in the nightclub.

In a fog of alcohol, without knowing how or why, Anja and I ended up in the tattoo parlor that night. Lying side by side on two beds, pants pulled down and finding it hard not to burst out laughing, we had our right buttocks decorated forevermore with a tattoo of a joyfully leaping dolphin.

Nevertheless, we still haven't come to the major changes I announced before. I said that the main character is Sam Cortina. And, as tends to happen when you take the risk of staking everything on a single card, the tattoo operation dampened our euphoria with overly sore buttocks. Anja and I decided we'd meet the next day and keep celebrating in a more intimate manner.

"After all, we're passengers on the Love Boat, aren't we?" She smiled from the door of her cabin, which she was about to enter alone, and kissed me. "Have a good night, Barbra," she said.

"Sweet dreams, Barry."

Though it was late, instead of going to bed, I decided to round off the night with a whisky sour in the Rimini. Moreover, in one of our earlier conversations when Sam and I were talking about music, we'd started praising the songs of Steely Dan, those two guys we both liked a lot, and I'd challenged him. Could he adapt "Deacon Blues" for piano and voice? He was going to perform it for the first time that night.

When I got to the Rimini, I had the impression that the other drinkers at the bar looked at me with some relief, as if confirming that, in the end, I hadn't let them down. The barman fixed my drink. On one of the sofas, entangled in the arms of a purser, I could see a squealing Marianne who sounded like she was getting ready for the fray. Sam ended his version of Cole Porter's "Night and Day" and, with some relish, set about "Deacon Blues." Breaking from his usual routine, he presented it as something new and dedicated it to me.

I couldn't imagine it then, but "Deacon Blues" was the last song I heard Sam Cortina sing. Those five minutes are absolutely unforgettable. I'm still fascinated by the whole thing, the song and that night in the Rimini. Standing at the bar, without being able to sit on a stool because of the emerging dolphin on my buttock, I heard how the piano notes stripped the Steely Dan melody of all its electricity and dressed it up again in a new, more fragile, moving rhythm. It was as if that song of the seventies had gone back forty years to end up in the hands of George Gershwin, let's say. I'd listened to the original dozens of times, but Sam's voice made some of the fragments stand out. "I play just what I feel / Drink Scotch whiskey all night long / And die behind the wheel / They got a name for the winners in the world / I want a name when I lose . . ." The words seemed to have been written solely for Sam. Claiming a name from his isolation.

When he finished "Deacon Blues," he took his usual break and came over to the bar. The barman served him his whisky without ice. Moved, I thanked him for his version, and when we shook hands, I could feel his whole arm trembling. The barman shot me a sideways look and raised his eyebrows. It was as if, when Sam sang that Steely Dan song, all sobriety had drained out of him, all the energy he had left.

He whispered in my ear, "Got a cig?" His breath stank of whisky and the words stumbled as they left his mouth.

"Let's go out on deck," I said. "We'll have a smoke and get some fresh air. You'll feel better up there."

On the deck, he recovered slightly in the cool night air. We were astern, leaning on the railing. The ship's engines churned up the water, leaving a whitish wake behind. We tossed our cigarette butts into it but they vanished in the dark before hitting the sea. Trying to revive him, because apparently he had to play again, I started talking to Sam about his adaptation and how he'd seemed to have taken over the song so easily and made it his. Then I asked if he composed any songs of his own. Among the covers he did, some were so free and personal that they sounded as if he'd written them himself.

"No," he said brusquely. But a few seconds later he cleared his throat, getting rid of a bad taste, and went on: "I don't write songs. I don't make records. I told you the other day, I live on this ship. In eight years, I've had my feet on the ground a dozen times and then only to go from one transatlantic liner to another and change the scenery a bit. And now I must say this, too: Atlantic or Mediterranean, it doesn't matter anymore. The sea's always the same when you sail on one of these monsters, and the people are, too."

"Can I ask why you're inflicting this penance on yourself?"

He hesitated a few seconds and reluctantly—it was evident—said, "Because of a woman."

"There's always a woman."

"And because of a song. But maybe it's the same thing in this case. Oh, and it's not punishment or penance, OK. As I see it, playing the piano every night is salvation. Look, I'm not a man of great ambition. Not anymore. There was a time when I thought I'd have the world at my feet. In the eighties, Las Vegas was the world for a pianist like me. One night some guys from a record label came and offered me a contract. The new Mark Murphy. Or, no, even better, the new Burt Bacharach, and that meant more money and more fame. I started composing, and the first song I wrote had a woman's name." At this point he paused and stared at me. An inner storm shimmered in his dull eyes. "First mistake: there are very few songs that survive a woman's name. Angie. Diana. Michelle. Suzanne. Aline, if you must. Then you can stop counting. Mistake number two was premiering it in public before recording it. I won't tell you her name. No need. I'd rehearsed it with a few guys in the casino orchestra and it sounded great. One especially brilliant night when my fingers were dancing over the keys and my voice was coming out with an intensity that had the public eating out of my hand—you can tell these things—I played it in one of the encores. We were at Caesars, the imperial colosseum, with an audience of nearly a thousand. She didn't know. It was a surprise for her. While we were playing, I was looking for her in the audience, in the place where she always sat, and I couldn't find her. Naturally. Because she was up in our casino hotel room packing her bag, taking everything with her. If she'd paid attention while she was stuffing my money into her luggage, she might almost have heard me singing out her name, declaring my love to the four winds. What happens in Vegas stays in Vegas, as I'm sure you've heard, and the weirdest things seem totally normal."

He went quiet again. He was woozy and clinging to the rail, trying to stay on his feet. He'd made several attempts to drain a few more drops of whisky from his empty glass. He was sweating and in the moonlight his skin had an unhealthy, pasty sheen.

The only thing I could come up with was "Life has many mysteries, Sam. You say you don't play your own songs and that you don't compose. Yet you make other people's songs your own. For example, nobody plays 'Yesterday' like you do."

"Steady, now. That's enough." He sounded as if he was calming a little boy he carried inside him but then let out a sarcastic laugh. Now he'd crossed some sort of line and couldn't get the words out straight. "I don't want to bore you anymore. We're getting bored, aren't we? Come on. The show must go on."

I took him at his word. He got down the stairway clinging to my back, staggering, and when we entered the Rimini it was evident that his legs were giving way under him. The barman came over and told me that "the accident" didn't happen very often but they'd been expecting this one for some days. Then he asked me if I'd take Sam to his cabin and gave me the number and a copy of the key.

The place where Sam Cortina had decided to bury his days wasn't much bigger than a first-class cabin. In any case it seemed smaller because some of the space was occupied by an upright piano wedged against the wall in case of rough seas and because the objects that, over the years, might have found a place there were strewn around in the utmost disorder, as if the ship had come through a tornado. I took off his shoes and got him to lie on the bed, on his side. In a couple of minutes he was snoring. I didn't want to snoop, but my admiration for the man led me to check out his belongings. A few signed photos hung on the walls. Among them I recognized Liza Minnelli, Dean Martin doffing his hat, and Petula Clark, who sent him a lot of kisses in the note she wrote. On the piano were several open scores, their pages coated in a film of cigarette ash. There was also a tape deck and a lot of recorded tapes, some of which were piled up outside their boxes, coexisting with a collection of mementos from cities where the cruiser berthed. The latter, bits of junk, looked very like gifts from some phony, spurious admirers. On the nightstand I found a picture frame with a Technicolor photo of a girl. It was slightly burned at the corners, had been ripped up and then very carefully stuck together again like a jigsaw puzzle. At first glance the girl, sitting in a typical diner, looking out at you with an adorable pose as if for some Pygmalion, seemed worthy of having a song written for her.

————

Sometimes I still wonder about the trophy that Anja and I won in the karaoke duets championship. She kept it. It was an ugly thing and I would have discreetly thrown it overboard one of those nights when the ship's routine, the programmed fun, weighed on you like a tombstone. Maybe she did that; who knows? Or maybe not. Maybe she keeps it as major booty—materialization of short-lived happiness—and it's decorating her house, on the mantelpiece over a Swedish fireplace. Her friends see it and read my name, Maury, and then Anja shows them the photo of the dinner and tells them cruise anecdotes while her husband struggles to suppress suspicious thoughts. But then again, they say Scandinavians see these things differently. Or maybe Sam Cortina ended up with it—which wouldn't be at all remarkable—and today it's gathering dust in his cabin next to all the other gifts that he doesn't know how to reject because he's a good man. And maybe the bottom line is that they keep him company. Oh, no, it wouldn't be at all surprising if Sam were now the guardian of the trophy.

The last day of the cruise, when we set sail from Marseille en route for Barcelona, I met up with Anja again. We had dinner together in the ship's most expensive restaurant, in candlelight, with jazz playing in the background. At some point in the conversation I told her about Sam Cortina and his songs. How he, this lonely guy, had made me homesick. After dinner and full of pride, I escorted her to the piano bar but Sam wasn't there. On the stand, beneath his name, a tired old poster announced in three languages that the pianist was indisposed that night. In order to get over our disappointment, Anja and I repaired to one of the sofas, where we smooched until our butt-dolphins started hurting. The barman and the usual barflies looked on incredulously. Before we said goodbye, I asked Anja to promise that one night after I was gone she'd go to the piano bar and ask Sam Cortina to play "Deacon Blues" for her.

Sometimes, when I come out of the shower and am alone in the bathroom, I look at my cavorting dolphin in the mirror. My wife knows I had it tattooed during my week of expiation on the *Wonderful Sirena*. I occasionally suggest that we should do a Mediterranean cruise, but she claims she wouldn't be caught dead on a ship with such a stupid name. It seems to me that she's afraid to discover what I experienced that week, or maybe she prefers not to know. Maybe I prefer it, too. But the thing is, I miss the tap dance fingers and velvet voice of Sam Cortina. What could have become of him?

MATTER

At first the movement is excruciatingly slow. He knows he has to open his eyelids and the world will gradually get going, like a turntable with the needle on a 45 rpm. The cracks composing his first view are random. There's no lineal order, no sequence he might have foreseen before closing his eyes. Sensorial perception is messily activated. He starts putting together the first details, now imposed in flashes that refuse to go away: car brakes squealing two meters from his ears; the repetitive cadence of traffic lights (like three-layered ice cream); a throbbing at his temple later reverberating in his pulse as a painful echo; the legs of passersby; unfolded newspapers; a child's crying; dry skin being scratched by fingernails; the hobble of a lame pigeon; the rough texture of the pavement beneath his buttocks; the smell of a warm croissant spreading over the ground mixed with his own piss . . . It seems impossible, but as the whole thing starts orchestrating and picks up the necessary tempo, the voices lose gravity and the background music is less opaque. The nausea's going away. Signals link up and sounds are sharper. Now he'd like to find some explanation for this mystery stubbornly binding him to life. Now he'd like to be ready, because the city will soon be a symphony of movements, a map of nerves, veins, muscles, and umbilical cords, and Lord knows where they start and where they end. By the time the revs get up to 45 and the urban music is echoing in the vault of his cranium, he's ready, too. He opens his eyes wide. He gets up, taking it slowly. He runs his fingers through greasy hair, tries to smooth over the eternal creases in his pullover and trousers and, while he's at it, dust off sleep. He takes two or three steps and then goes back. He seems to be exploring the two square meters where he's slept. He tries to get his bearings, reconstruct the world. He puts his hand in his pocket and his fingers recoil in horror: he finds a knot of cloth that could be covering anything, but he can't remember what. Right now everything is possible: a few walnuts, half a dozen coins, a dead bird, a live mouse. Someone walking by curses and the incomprehensible words make him stagger. To calm down, he joins his fingers as if praying and passes them over his belly. This trick always works. But it's early in the day and now his stomach's telling him it's hungry. He's not sure whether to take another step or stay where he is, and his feet, which don't always obey, move in opposite directions, four steps of an impromptu tap dance. He stays where he is because a flash of sunlight dazzles him. It's then that, without warning, a mute shudder sets out from the deepest depths of his being, an expansive wave rising until it finally comes out of his mouth. Now, yes, he does take two steps forward, opens out his arms, making the shape of a cross, and there, in the middle of the street, as if everyone has to celebrate this instant of a morning epiphany, he yells at the top of his lungs, "Matter obeys God!"

———

A fragment of his map. The corner of Passeig de Sant Joan and Provença, Barcelona. After paying the bill Daniel methodically distributes his purchases into two bags. With practiced speed, he puts the heaviest things like the pack of tonic water bottles and balsamic vinegar at the bottom and, on top of them, a tender layer of greens—a lettuce, arugula, and a bag of cherry tomatoes—to cushion the journey of the pâté, the sausages and cheeses. Every movement he makes is loving, as if the food understands the important role it will have in a few hours' time and therefore demands special treatment. Tonight, Daniel and Carola are going to celebrate their tenth anniversary of living together. It will be an improvised feast at home, because their son's babysitter let them down at the last minute, but they've accepted the change of plan without much fuss and even a certain youthful excitement. After calling the restaurant to cancel their reservation, they planned a menu that would be up to the occasion. In the supermarket Daniel hasn't stinted on their dinner—always cheaper than the restaurant, he told himself—and, carried away by euphoria, he even bought two bottles of French champagne.

So, with the weight balanced between the two bags, Daniel leaves the supermarket and, back in the street, is surprised to see that it's getting dark. Last Saturday they switched back to standard time and he still hasn't adapted to the hours of fall. Beneath the amber glow of the streetlamps the atmosphere is clear but sparkly, as if rain isn't far away. *Barcelona, too, gets sadder in the fall,* he thinks as he watches a boy and girl kissing in a doorway. A few steps farther on, he once again notices the hobo in his usual place on the corner. The man rouses in Daniel an irrational feeling of apprehension. He's never done or said anything untoward, but his presence is unsettling. Tall, unkempt, with thick greasy hair, big prominent cheekbones, and patchy whiskers suggesting that he's shaved without a mirror, he's there all day long, lying in an unnatural position. If it wasn't for his eyes, violently scrutinizing everything around him, you'd think he didn't have long to live.

It should be said that the hobo isn't a permanent fixture. Sometimes he disappears from his corner and doesn't come back for several days. Since he doesn't look especially shabby—he always wears a baggy old-fashioned suit in herringbone weave, the cloth stiffened with age and stains—Daniel can't help being reminded of his father, who he visits in the nursing home every Sunday. He has the same look of neglect and helpless air. Daniel always leaves both of them behind with the absurd impression that they're plotting something and, worse, something bad.

It's possible that the withdrawn character of the vagrant on the corner encourages comparison. He never asks for a handout, although he accepts the offerings of some local residents who give him money or food. He spends hours on end leafing through newspapers and magazines he finds in nearby trash cans, and classifying the scraps he's torn out. This silent, introverted world changes only occasionally and without warning. Like now. Daniel is walking with his bags, approaching the crosswalk. Suddenly the man stands up, extends his arms in the form of a cross, stares ahead at some indefinite place, and bellows as loud as he can, "Matter obeys God!"

He repeats it three more times, turning in the direction of each cardinal point. Then he lies down again on his patch of sidewalk. Daniel hears the words and repeats them in his head. *Matter obeys God.* He recalls having heard them before, some months ago, but now he's trying to find some meaning in them. First, or so he muses, thought is lost in the dense construction of the statement, in the declaration of religious faith it implicitly bears; but by the time he gets in the elevator, a neighbor has definitively distracted him with a few platitudes about the bad weather that's on its way.

––––

When he opens the door of the apartment, Daniel can smell the fragrance of kids' shampoo coming from the bathroom. Sometimes, when he's having his shower in the morning, he's so sleepy, he picks it up by mistake and then the cloying sweetness is with him all day. When he feels hassled in the office, he rolls up his sleeve and sniffs his arm to get back the familiar soothing smell.

"Hi, it's me," he calls, leaving his keys on the tray.

A double answer issues from the bathroom.

"Hi! All well?" Carola asks.

"Hi! All well?" Àlvar, his five-year-old son, asks two seconds later.

"Yes, yes. All well," Daniel answers. He goes into the kitchen, sets out the shopping on the table, then moves things into the fridge and hides one of the bottles of champagne in the freezer behind the spinach.

He wants it to be a surprise for Carola. He opens a bottle of red, pours two glasses, and leaves them on the marble bench so the wine can breathe. Taking off his shoes, jacket, and tie in the dressing room next to the bedroom, he can hear Àlvar splashing in the bath and Carola's delighted laugh. Àlvar must be playing, fooling around, and putting on an act for her, maybe wearing his goggles to keep the soap out of his eyes. Trying not to make any noise, he tiptoes to the bathroom and peeps through the slightly open door. Then he sees that Carola's in the bathtub with Àlvar. He didn't expect this and feels a small stab of jealousy. Since it's not yet Àlvar's dinnertime, he quietly starts undressing. The tub is large and circular. There's enough room for three. As he's taking off his underpants he hears Carola telling Àlvar they'll have to get out soon. Daniel hurries. He makes his triumphal entry before it's too late, planning to get in the bathtub, too. The mirror is misted in steam. Carola smiles and her face shines in the haze. Probably she's reminded of one of those evenings before they had Àlvar when they used to get in the tub together. Candles, a glass of wine, bath salts in the water, love and slippery sex. Just as Daniel's about to get in the water, Àlvar takes off his goggles—also fogged over—and sees his father.

"No-o-o!" he shouts. "Not you!"

Daniel has no place in his son's aquatic kingdom. Carola scolds naughty Àlvar—she likes the image of the three of them together in the tub—and he begins to whimper. With one foot in the water, Daniel's not sure whether he should get in or retreat, and feels ridiculous. He's a little cold and in the end decides to get in. Àlvar cries louder.

"Now it's not even lukewarm. It's more like cold," Carola warns, and turns on the hot-water tap. Since his parents are ignoring him, Àlvar wipes away his tears with his hands and gets soap in his eyes, which start stinging, so now he's really bawling, with a lot of feeling this time. The blissful harmony that reigned in the bathroom a moment ago has evaporated. Carola gives up. With a brusque movement she swishes out of the water, lifts Àlvar out too, and unceremoniously bundles him in a towel. As she dries his hair, the crying is muffled and calm seems to return. Lying in the bathtub, Daniel looks at her naked body, smooth skin, gleaming wet back, little ribbons of foam scattered on her ass. Right now, this evening, this anniversary Friday, the image is exciting. He turns off the tap. He wants to masturbate but desists because of the presence of his son and the prospect of the sex that will come later, after dinner. He looks up and finds Carola observing him from the mirror with a hint of a smile.

When mother and son leave him alone, Daniel listens to the silence that enfolds him. His mind links up several ideas. He slides under the water and says, "Matter obeys God." The words disintegrate in a string of bubbles rising to the surface. Daniel holds his breath while he counts to forty, and when he can't keep counting anymore, he sticks his head out again. An explosion of air.

———

Àlvar got over his tantrum, made peace with his father, and dropped off to sleep when they were reading a story. Now alone in the dining room, Carola and Daniel toast their anniversary with French champagne. Since they never married, they chose as the date for their celebration the first night they slept together under a shared roof, the day Daniel moved into Carola's apartment. They met as students in the fine arts faculty. In their shared prehistory they'd both chosen to do Russian cinematography. Coming out from screenings of Eisenstein or Pudovkin, they'd go off to the faculty bar with some of their classmates and amuse themselves with smart-ass analysis in an improvised movie forum. Then everyone went home and, in the subway, Daniel and Carola translated all those glances, gestures, discussions, and visceral understanding into the language of love. Having got past the phase of tentative approaches and now dating, their interests began to diverge. Carola focused on history of art, especially sculpture, while Daniel toned down his ideas about moviemaking to channel them into the more predictable world of television. The professional estrangement only increased after Àlvar was born. Shortly beforehand, when she was already pregnant, they agreed that Daniel should accept a very attractive offer from a production company famous for lightweight, provocative programs. Carola would stay home to look after the baby and use her spare time to make some progress with her never-ending doctoral dissertation on sculpture and landscape. In the end, as tends to happen, she didn't have much free time and the baby absorbed all her energy. Daniel, however, found in his job—project analyst specializing in new formats—an escape from the pressures of his newly acquired paternity.

They open the second bottle of French champagne. The sparkle of the bubbles has shifted to Carola's eyes. When they reach this point, Daniel always gazes at her adoringly. Watching her talk, he thinks they should carry the glasses and bottle off to the bedroom and finish the party there. But he's not sure whether Carola would want that. Today might be an exception, but the thing is, for a while now, when they do decide to fuck, he's sensed something ambivalent or elusive about her. Sometimes he worries that she suspects he's having an affair with someone from the office. (He's not but is tempted by the possibility, although none has arisen so far.) Perhaps that's why, instead of hinting that they should fall into bed, he waits for her to make the first move and, meanwhile, starts telling her about the vagrant on the corner, saying that he's seen him again today.

"I don't know, but sometimes I think the guy's dangerous," Daniel says, but then realizes that he's exaggerating. "No. Rather than dangerous, he's intriguing. With that thing he sometimes shouts, 'Matter obeys God' . . . You know, at work, I've met more than one of these screwballs. They're unpredictable, and often the day comes when they'll do something really crazy."

"Well, I think exactly the opposite," Carola says. "I often have a good look at him when I'm going past and I always get the feeling he's trying to tell us something—that he wants to ask for help but can't find the words. One of these days I'm going to stop and talk to him, to see what he'll say."

"No, don't do that," Daniel hastens to say. He knows his tone is too sharp and disagreeable, so repeats himself more gently: "No, don't, please. You won't get anything out of it. It's blindingly obvious that he's a nutcase. He just needs someone to provoke him . . . Heaven knows what's going on in his head."

"And that's supposed to be a problem?" Carola's indignant. "Are you trying to say this doesn't happen to everyone? You, for example. Sometimes I haven't got a clue what you're thinking . . ."

"Don't compare," he says. Now he's silently cursing himself for mentioning the hobo.

———

In Socrates, Pennsylvania, there's a sculpture park funded by a millionaire philanthropist. In an area covering several acres of forestland, the wild vegetation has to coexist with a series of works of art created for this place. The foundation's catalog explains that "the sculptures aim to blend with nature, create visual violence, or simply question man's influence on the landscape." In one of the park's fields, the visitor tends to stop before a work in granite, more or less oval in shape and about the same size as a sack of potatoes. At first, from a distance, it's difficult to see whether it's a work of art or just a big rock that predates the sculptures, but then it turns out that, balanced on top of the rock, is another, smaller one, golden in color and the size of a melon: this one's pyrite. Ever since it was installed in that corner of the park, rain and general exposure to the elements have been working on the pyrite's mineral content and whittling the granite, carving out new furrows in its matter and changing its color. The piece is called "No Wishes, 1983" and is the work of an American sculptor called William Bartholomew, known to his friends as Bill. In the nineteen eighties, thanks to the good offices of a well-connected art dealer, Bartholomew managed to get his work placed in quite a lot of the most prestigious museums and private contemporary art collections. Far from going to his head, success drove him to paring down his genius into ever more primal forms. He abandoned his family, moved to an isolated mountain region, and kept working in solitude. One day, after a long silence, he disappeared from the cabin where he'd been living. Then there was no more news of him. The story was published in arty magazines and was a theme of the Kassel documenta that year. Some artists idolized him for his stand, which they almost certainly understood as voluntary and extreme.

Recently, every time she sees the man on the corner, Carola thinks of William Bartholomew. Her argument with Daniel last Friday, his intransigence, has made her return to her old projects, and this Monday morning she's set about trying to glean more information about the artist. After spending quite a while trawling through her thesis files, she finds some photocopies of an American art magazine. The article gives an account of the artist's disappearance and suggests that, in the final analysis, this could be his last work, the ultimate gesture in his zeal to explore the connection between matter, being, and nothingness. The text offers a biographical note and is illustrated with a few photos of William Bartholomew. Carola studies them carefully. They're more than twenty years old, and the dark tones of the photocopy make them look slightly scorched, but this could certainly be the man on the corner. His face has a fugitive look about it. Excited, she reads the biographical note again. Among other things, it says that Bartholomew was hospitalized as an adolescent after some psychotic episodes—he'd been experimenting with LSD—and, toward the end of his creative life, as part of his general evolution, he'd become a radical vegetarian, a vegan. One of the very few friends who visited him occasionally said he only ate raw vegetables—garlic, onions, tomatoes, and bell peppers he grew in his garden—and he recycled his urine and feces as fertilizer.

Carola suddenly feels full of pity for the man. She goes

out onto the balcony, looking for him on the corner, below her, through the trees. In the space between the newsstand and the traffic lights, she sees his curled-up legs. She stays there for some minutes. The man gets up and takes a few steps. Now he's in her field of vision. He goes over to the traffic lights and looks up at the sky. If he turned, he'd see her. But he doesn't. Carola keeps staring until the lanky figure melts into the gray ether of the city. By the time she has him back in focus, he's lying in his spot on the corner again.

Carola goes to collect Àlvar from preschool in the afternoon. If Daniel can leave work on time, it's usually his job to get him, but today he's called to say he won't be home until evening. The producer has started choosing the new participants for one of those competitions starring freaks, misfits, and lunatics, the kind with huge audiences, and he has to go to the studios to supervise the selection. Carola and Àlvar reach the hobo's corner. (Deep inside, without really being aware of it, she's started calling him Bill.) He's sitting there in his stronghold, legs crossed and absorbed in tearing out photos from a newspaper. He keeps turning the pages, and when he finds an image he likes, he folds the page several times until the picture is framed, and then dampens the edges with his tongue so it tears straight. When he's finished with one of the images, he folds it again and puts it in his jacket pocket. This afternoon, a little thicket of bits of paper is peeping over the top of his pocket like a scrunched-up handkerchief. Carola misses no detail of the operation. She'd like to take a look at the pictures that attract him and try to find some sense in it all. Àlvar tugs at her hand, wanting to go home. She opens her bag, takes out a twenty-euro bill, and asks him to give it to the gentleman. Àlvar fearlessly goes over to the stranger and holds out the money, but the man, still absorbed by his bits of paper, seems not to have seen him. Àlvar moves closer and squats beside him. The man squints at him briefly but keeps turning the pages of a newspaper. Carola is still rooted to the spot. Then Àlvar does something surprising: he moves still closer to the man, puts his hand in one of the deep, dark, dirty pockets of his trousers, and leaves the money there. Carola shivers. "Àlvar, come here," she says sweetly. "Don't bother the gentleman."

The man stands up, as if Àlvar has activated some inner mechanism, but his attitude isn't aggressive or pained. It's more like slow-dawning surprise. When he moves, his clothes give off a sour, rank smell, and Àlvar covers his nose and goes back to his mother.

"Hello," she says. "My name is Carola and this is my son, Àlvar. Would you like to come up to our place? *Vol pujar a casa nostra?*" She says it in English and Catalan, to be sure.

"Why?" he asks. His voice is higher than you'd expect.

"To have a bath in our bathtub." Àlvar beats her to it. "You smell."

———

The man without a name still isn't answering any questions. When they move off, he meekly follows, leaving on his patch of sidewalk a sheaf of newspapers and a trash bag full of whatever it is, and which nobody would dare to touch. At the entrance of their building, the janitor greets them with some misgiving and asks if everything is all right. Carola nods with a reassuring smile. They go up in the elevator without saying a word, and, once inside the apartment, the man follows Carola's instructions, goes into the bathroom, and closes the door. Half an hour later, wearing the same dirty clothes but with his hair combed and smelling of Àlvar's shampoo, he comes out and wanders around the apartment looking for them. They are in the kitchen. Àlvar is eating a potato omelet and, on seeing her guest, Carola asks if he wants some. He shakes his head. A few minutes go by and he just stands there, as if taking in what's happened so far.

Àlvar keeps eating, his attention captured by a children's program on television as his mother feeds him small bits of omelet. Carola's head is seething with questions rehearsed a hundred times, but when she tries to get them out, they crash against the granitic expression of the nameless man before they leave her mouth. Gradually, like a magnetic pole, his silent, static presence is exerting its power over everything around them. And what if time has stopped? No, that's not possible, Carola thinks. A few more minutes go by. Then, without warning, the man moves his arm and grabs the remote control.

As he's seen Àlvar do, he starts pressing the different buttons. Television channels flip by and in no time a rhythm is born. The screen keeps blinking. At first he never stays on one channel for more than five seconds. Then he lingers longer. Ten seconds, twenty, thirty. Carola watches, fascinated. Àlvar starts sniveling.

"Matter obeys God," the nameless man mumbles.

"What are you saying, Bill? What does that mean?" Carola asks.

Silence. He looks at her for a second and then concentrates again on the screen, as if he wants to tell her that the answer's in the television. One channel follows upon another. In his mind, words and images mingle to create sense. Everything is becoming ordered. It seems that he's been waiting years for this moment. His face, jaw, and cheeks relax. He takes some of the torn-out photographs from his pocket and spreads them on the table. Everything's becoming ordered more quickly. He points the remote control at the photos and presses the buttons. Àlvar sobs and sobs but doesn't appear to be suffering. It's more like an unconscious reaction, as if he, too, were part of the game. Carola shuffles the photographs. Maybe that will help him to find some rhythmic sequence in the images. The hands of the nameless man, or Bill, or whatever he's called, stop moving and he closes his eyes. You'd think he knows what's going to happen in the future.

———

So let's see what's going to happen quite soon. Daniel will come home from work. He'll open the door of the apartment and find the three of them in the kitchen. Àlvar, who will have stopped crying, will hug him. Carola will smile and tell him that their guest is a famous sculptor who disappeared many years ago. Daniel will take the remote control from the nameless man, turn off the television, and call the police, but at the last minute he'll change his mind and hang up. Then he'll take the vagrant to the elevator, out into the street, and escort him to his corner. Carola will be very angry. The days will go by. Daniel might have an affair at work after all. Some mornings, while she's working on her thesis, Carola will have the urge to go out on the balcony to see if Bill's on his corner. But he won't be there. More days will go by without any sign of life from Bill. One night, the new program produced by Daniel will be premiered. Àlvar will be in bed asleep—he's going to have nightmares—and Carola will be sitting alone in front of the television. The program is called *I See, I See* and she'll soon discover that it is, in fact, a competition for seers. In the first round tonight, two contestants compete to get on the next program, convinced they're on the way to getting a place in the grand finale. A *meiga* from Galicia who says she can see the future in the sheets and blankets of an unmade bed is challenged by a solemn, enigmatic gentleman who has a highly original method for predicting the future: interpreting a series of images obtained by random surfing through TV channels. Viewers will be able to vote for him by sending messages on their cell phones. They only have to dial the number 7878 and then write "*I See, I See* Mr. Matter."

THE MIRACLE OF
THE LOAVES AND THE FISHES

Not long ago, one afternoon at the beginning of summer, I
ran into my friend Miquel Franquesa, who now calls himself Mike. Saying he's a friend is probably an exaggeration,
because in fact we've seen each other just a couple of times
in three years, but it's also true that our contact was never
only sporadic and casual but has involved the exact degree
of trust and perhaps intimacy—especially on his side—
resulting from shared money.

I say I ran into him, but actually he was the one who
saw me first. I was walking along Passeig Marítim toward
La Barceloneta, when someone coming in the opposite
direction stopped in front of me and blocked my way with a
smile. It took me almost ten seconds to recognize that face,
the time I needed to salvage it from memory and understand

that it had aged and was the worse for wear. I greeted him, trying to mask my surprise. The Miquel I'd met three years earlier had been thin, if anything, was well into his thirties, with gentle evasive features and a ferrety look about him. His laid-back cheerfulness was emphasized by the fact that his shirt was nearly always half hanging out. But the Mike who was now standing before me reminded me of a boiled fish, a salmon, swollen and flabby rather than fat, his skin sporting an orangey tan. He was wearing a Yankees cap, a stain-spattered sky-blue polo shirt tucked into his jeans, and multihued sneakers.

We shook hands and exchanged a few polite words of greeting. His voice sounded less anxious than I remembered it, as if well tuned by tranquilizers. He said it was more than six months since he'd come back for Christmas holidays and had decided to stay, although everyone had advised him not to. Bloody crisis. But he'd even found work.

"So I guess you're on your way to the casino," I ventured with a touch of mischief, because we were nearby and that was where we'd first met.

"Yes," he said, "but it's not what you think. I stopped gambling. Now I work there."

I must have given him an incredulous look, because he then invited me to have a beer with him. So, while he'd have something to eat, we'd have a long chat and caught up on each other's news. His shift didn't start for another hour and a half.

Miquel told me that, in those three years, he'd traveled thousands of miles and had met dozens of people.

He'd had an ardent lover and had managed to escape in the nick of time from the perils personified by the cuckolded husband. He'd propelled a gondola through the canals of Venice, had driven a Ferrari, and had been tempted by the idea of killing himself by jumping off the Eiffel Tower. In the end he'd always survived. Maybe that's the word that best captures the ups and downs of his life. In spite of himself, he was a survivor. And now he was back in Barcelona. Before I get into his story, though, it's worth recalling how we met . . .

Let's begin, perhaps, by saying that Miquel was a regular at the Barcelona casino. In August 2008 I was writing a novel and had decided that I needed some cardplayers in an important chapter. For days I'd been struggling with the scene in which I had to describe a poker game. I knew how to do the atmosphere but couldn't get the players' expressions when they first see their cards, their faces during an especially tense round, the complacent silence of the winner, knowing he's cheated . . . One very hot Friday evening, then, I headed off to the casino to watch the blackjack players and, while I was there, enjoy the air-conditioning. I know myself and, since I'm a sucker when it comes to games of chance, I left my credit cards at home and took only sixty euros in case I was tempted to play.

Once I got inside the casino, my plan to watch the card players became an unfulfilled wish. Blackjack games were off-limits to the public. The tables were cloistered away from the rest of the room by a discreet wooden partition and a security guard who let in only accredited players. For a few seconds I wondered whether I should go back home, but the comfortable feel of the casino and the heady, roiling atmosphere you breathe when money's at stake kept me there a while longer. I asked for a gin and tonic and, with the glass in my hand, strolled around the roulette tables as if I owned the place. (Yes, I've seen a lot of movies.) It was then that, at one of the tables with more people gathered round it, I noticed Miquel Franquesa for the first time. His body-and-soul surrender to the game fascinated me, and, trapped in this magnetic field, I couldn't take my eyes off him for over an hour. In which time he lost everything.

I don't know how much money it was, though I figured it was close to two thousand euros, but not a flicker crossed his face. In the end, when he lost his last chip and the croupier languidly swept it into his territory, I noted a small grimace of disgust but nothing more than that. He got up, waved at nobody in particular, and left. Naturally, I followed, and saw him going into one of the restrooms. I went in too and, trying to look as if I wasn't tailing him, went to wash my hands. After pissing, he came over to wash his.

"So you feel sorry for me, huh?" he asked from the mirror.

"No," I said. "I'm impressed. How can you lose so much, just like that?"

"Bad luck. It's always bad luck. Luck comes and goes. I played 12 all afternoon because today's the twelfth, and as you saw, I lost every time. But if we went back now and bet on 12, there's nothing to indicate that we'd lose again."

"Or that we'd win either . . . ," I suggested.

"Exactly. Shall we try? Do you have some money on you?"

I left his invitation hanging in the air for a few seconds, long enough to dry my hands under a rasping dryer. Since I hadn't quite decided, Miquel repeated his question, now with a slightly different slant. "Do you have some money on you? Will you lend it to me?"

"Yes, I do. Fifty euros. But you won't get far with fifty euros."

"You're wrong about that," he said. "As I see the game, fifty euros hold out the promise of more loot. You only have to know how to *work them* and luck will be with you. It's like when Michelangelo stood in front of a block of marble and saw what there was inside. David, Moses . . ."

"No, man, it's not really the same thing," I objected, but I admit I was amused by the comparison and was therefore indulgent. He must have noticed, because he tried again. "Lend me the fifty euros and we'll go halves. Or, better still, lend me fifty euros and I'll give you a hundred back. Which would be tomorrow. A twenty-four-hour loan at a hundred percent. It's a great offer."

He was so persuasive, I couldn't resist. I shrugged and gave him the fifty-euro bill. He quickly stuffed it in his wallet as though the money might burn his fingers or bring bad luck just by looking at it and thanked me with a trusting, almost comradely look. We left the restroom together and I followed him to the gaming table, but after a few steps Miquel turned and said he'd see me the next day. It was a polite way of saying he didn't want me there, that lending him the money didn't give me the right to watch him gamble it, my investment in his talent, so I left convinced I'd never see my fifty euros again.

The next day, however, curiosity drove me back to the casino at the same hour. Miquel was waiting for me outside. He was wearing sunglasses as if trying to cover up the tiredness on his face.

"No need to go in," he said, handing me two fifty-euro bills.

"Well, I'll be damned. I didn't expect that. So you got on a winning streak . . ."

"No, hell no, I lost everything," he admitted with a rueful smile, "but I'm a man of my word. Thanks to your fifty euros, I played for more than four hours and made myself a nice little fortune, about a thousand euros, but I couldn't stop, so I ended up losing the whole lot again. That's life for you."

I now understood that, as well as being a man of his word, Miquel Franquesa was impetuous, stubborn, and hooked on the adrenaline of impulse, even if it meant his own perdition. To round off the clinical report, he was also a dauntless optimist, the sort who'd dive into a swimming pool without checking to see if there's water in it. I looked at him and, feeling sorry for him, tried to return one of the two bills, but he wouldn't accept it. On the contrary: he turned serious and told me that I'd inadvertently earned the money. My fortuitous intercession had been "therapeutic and enriching" (his words). Then he told me that, going home in a taxi, crushed and with empty pockets, he'd had an epiphany. The taxi driver was listening to the radio, one of those light-entertainment programs talking about Catalans scattered round the world. Then the presenter had said there were about a hundred of our compatriots living in Las Vegas, "capital of gambling and endless entertainment." Miquel took that as a challenge. If he wanted to stop gambling for good, the best place to kick the habit was Las Vegas.

"Are you serious?" I dared to interrupt.

"Absolutely. There's nothing like getting burned to keep you away from fire for the rest of your life."

Once again, I thought his example was far-fetched, but I could see that his eyes were shining with an excitement so pure, I'd almost call it faith, and, anyway, I had no right to question his decision. Moreover, he was all ready to go. That morning he'd withdrawn the few savings he had left, sold his laptop at a ridiculously low price (after saving all his documents on a flash drive), placed an online ad to rent his apartment, and got a ticket to fly to Las Vegas in three days' time. One way only.

"Thanks a lot. I'm really grateful," Miquel said, clutching my hand with unhealthy sincerity as we took our leave. "Thanks for everything."

I watched him walk away, determined, an explorer with a mission. Then, maybe in homage to his guts or his folly, I went into the casino and lost the hundred euros he'd given me.

As I said before, Miquel now calls himself Mike. This pared-down name, which seems essential for understanding his character today, was a product of his life in the United States. When I met him on Passeig Marítim, it was as if that raw enthusiasm of three years earlier had shrunk to nothing in the daily reality of Las Vegas, yet the words came out of him without the slightest sign of bitterness or remorse.

"Las Vegas is everything you want," he continued as we savored the cold beer, "and, what's more, it's never-ending. I guess you know that sociologists tend to refer to it as a non-place. Yeah, well, it is, but it's also a non-time. The hours go by any old how and often you can't tell day from night. Outside, it's always light, whether it's the glare of the desert sun or thousands of lit-up signs decorating the city after nightfall. If you haven't seen a rosy sunset sky profiled against the green neon lights of the MGM Grand Hotel, you haven't seen anything. And inside the casinos there are no clocks, so time slips away or stops, depending on the mood of the game."

The reference to casinos made me raise my eyebrows.

"Yeah, right, I know. You'll find this difficult to believe, but I didn't set foot in a gaming room until six months after I landed in Las Vegas," he explained. "Outside the famous Strip, which everyone knows from the movies, behind the showy decoration, there's a city made of houses that look like prefab, all of them almost exactly the same, spreading out into nowhere. When I arrived, I found a cheap motel, the Blue Cockatoo, and stayed there for two weeks. Just for the thrill of it, I registered under a false name, Mike

Picasso, and the receptionist didn't bat an eyelid. Good sign. I had a tourist visa, but my intention was to find a job so as not to use up my savings too fast. I could describe the motel now, the king-size bed, the swimming pool with greenish water (always with a plastic ball bobbing around), the ice maker in the corridor, the drifters like myself, the sexual feats, the nighttime battles on the other side of the thin wall, almost certainly over money. But I won't. You can imagine it for yourself."

"I can imagine it very well. You're right."

"The first five days I didn't leave the motel," he went on. "I was overwhelmed by everything. I could hear the constant buzzing of the city out there, could see the lights from my window, and I told myself I wasn't ready to face it. I spent hours in the pool, lounging about in a deck chair, eating only fries and chili chicken wings, which I had sent up to my room. From my open-air observation post I could monitor the casino losers coming and going, leaving in the morning with hope written on their faces and stumbling back at night as human wreckage.

"The fifth day I got up feeling stronger, as if completely cured of my gambling habit. I felt that I was part of that world, no longer a raw recruit, and that with my self-imposed abstinence I'd earned the right to live there. Then it struck me: I didn't know where to start."

"If I remember rightly, you were going there to look for Catalans . . ."

"Yeah, well, that was just an excuse, but it's true it worked for me in the end. One morning I took a free shuttle bus to the Bellagio fountains, which are spectacular, and then walked along the Strip: Caesars Palace, Bally's, the Tropicana . . . mythical names I'd heard a thousand times, offered up to me as a temptation . . . And, man, this was really temptation. It's a gambler's paradise. Luckily I was clear about my objective. I watched the people going in and leaving and sometimes when they walked by I sang "Baixant de la font del gat" or "El meu avi" out loud, in case one of those Catalans apparently residing in Las Vegas heard me warbling on about walking down from the cat's fountain or my dear old granddad. But no luck. No one took the bait. Then, just when I was about to give up, someone called out, 'Hey, Catalan! *Barcelona és bona si la bossa sona . . .*' I turned around. Barcelona's good if your pocket jingles as it should. Who'd come out with that old saying? He was an elegantly dressed bearded guy, of Cuban origin and the grandson of Catalans whom he'd heard singing *havaneres*—the Catalan-Cuban-African version of the old English-French contredanse—when he was a kid. His name was Bonany and he was doing a balancing act on Rollerblades at the exit of one of the casinos, handing out leaflets trying to convince the clients to forget about gambling for a while and go to see the musical *Les Misérables*. I invited him to a slice of pizza, basically to have someone to talk to, and told him I was looking for work but not sure how to go about it. 'Well, you found the right man, bro,' he claimed. 'But let me ask: Can you speak Spanish with a Latino accent?' I said I could, that I could imitate Mexicans, Argentines, and maybe Venezuelans. The next day I had my first job in Las Vegas. Not legal, naturally."

———

Mike Franquesa went on to tell me that he earned his first wages parking cars in one of the second-class casinos. It turned out that Wilfredo Bonany, the part-Catalan, part-Cuban guy he'd just met, had set up a business giving work to illegal immigrants. In Las Vegas, like everywhere else, there are smaller casinos, parasite businesses living off gambling, getting by behind the front line, in the shadow of the big empires. They're ideal places to make your way when you've just arrived and aren't aiming high. And no one asks awkward questions. Wilfredo Bonany's strategy was very simple yet closely studied: he wanted good-looking young folk in their thirties from Latin America and newly arrived in Las Vegas. And better still if their English was basic, as was the case with Mike Franquesa. Wilfredo went to the job interviews, dressed in his own distinctive way, big, bushy beard and all, responding shyly and with a reserved demeanor helped by his apparent difficulties with the language. Then he produced his totally legal documents proving he was a citizen and normally got the job. Basic unskilled labor. On the first day Wilfredo sent along some other bro, as he put it, having instructed him to show up clean-shaven and to be reserved at all times, like he'd been at the interview.

Thanks to this tactic, based on uniforms and, in particular, the inability of human resources managers to distinguish between the faces and accents of Latin Americans, Wilfredo Bonany had a staff of a dozen people who worked for him in his name, and in exchange they gave him thirty percent of their salary. Slippery as an eel, he was a kind of temp-to-hire agency for gardeners, cleaners, food delivery guys, valet parking attendants, and so on. He had a good eye for business and covered all kinds of work. He only had to be careful not to sign more than one contract per company. The ubiquitous discretion of business in Las Vegas did the rest.

In Mike's case, everything happened as Bonany had planned. Since he was working the night shift, on his first day he arrived at the casino at six in the afternoon. His boss asked about the beard and, following Bonany's instructions, he said he'd shaved it off to give a good impression, which instantly got him points. He was given a uniform and introduced to the guy who did the same shift, an Armenian of crabbed character and twitchy movements who had to show him how to go about parking cars.

"I worked there for eight months," Mike Franquesa recalled as we asked for a second beer and he checked out the menu. "It was very boring but a good apprenticeship for understanding the ins and outs of Las Vegas social life, the codes that separated those who work and those who are out for a good time. We parked cars for people who wanted to go to the casino or a complex of restaurants vaguely modeled on New York, with pizzerias, hamburger joints, taco stalls . . . Always in the shadow of a sheepish-looking reproduction of the Statue of Liberty and a papier-mâché arch that was supposed to resemble the ones of Brooklyn Bridge. My job was to open the car doors, politely greet the clients, and then drive their vehicles round the block to an underground parking lot. There, two security guards wrote down the license plate in a register, and when one of the cars was reclaimed, they gave us back the keys so we could return it to its owner. We were running up and down all night without many breaks, and if I say it was a boring job, it's because most of the cars were hired at the airport and total dullsville; but once in a while a Maserati, say, or a Ferrari or a Lamborghini showed up and the Armenian and I discreetly scrapped over who'd get to drive them. And, man, those five minutes at the wheel! He had more experience, of course, but sometimes I got to drive one of those marvels. More than once, when I'd gotten into a Ferrari, for example, I could have hit the accelerator to give free rein to the thoroughbred, to get the hell out of there, racing through the Las Vegas night, past the boulevard, to lose myself forever. If I didn't do it, it's because it would have brought me bigger problems. Where the city ends, the desert begins, and the desert is enormous and terrifying. Then again, there was the question of tips. The better the car and the more spectacular the alpha male's bevy of beauties, the more disposed he was to impress them by forking out a good tip. And those extra bucks, of course, were very attractive, because they didn't count in Wilfredo Bonany's thirty percent."

At this point Mike Franquesa went quiet for a moment as if trying to summon up the silence of the desert at sundown, as if wondering whether to tell me about some dramatic aspect of his story; so, to prod him a bit, I obligingly asked what other jobs he'd done apart from parking cars.

"Well, now," he said, "the casino folk gave us one day off a week, but Bonany often used that to relocate us when someone unexpectedly left or was out sick. We were a kind of army of Latino clones at his service. So that's how I got to work several times as a gondolier at the Venetian, a fabulous aberration of a place. My job was to take the gondolier round the casino's canals, where water and sky were animation-movie blue. Every ten minutes I had to start singing "O sole mio" and stop at the fake Bridge of Sighs because a couple of hicks from Texas, Ohio, or Nebraska wanted to have a photo taken and a kiss, in that order. Among my other jobs were cleaning the swimming pool at the Las Vegas Country Club, being an Egyptian waiter at the Luxor casino, and picking up cartridges and changing targets at a seedy rifle range. But, anyway, all these occupations were satellites of the parking job, and that ended very badly . . ."

"Oh, yeah? Why?"

"Some Catalans were to blame. How about that? One night I was attending to two middle-aged couples in a car that had been hired at the airport, as I'd done so many times before. One of the women stared at me and, when her husband was giving me the car keys, blurted out, 'You're Miquel, aren't you? Mireia's cousin?' I looked up in surprise. I couldn't restrain myself, so—as Catalans do when they're out in the big world—I said yes, I was, greeted them, and then we started looking for connections. They were friends of my cousin Mireia. We hardly knew each other, had only run into each other at the odd summer party, but I made the most of the occasion and had a good long chat with them. It was months since I'd spoken Catalan, and I had trouble finding the words. After a while we said goodbye and arranged to meet up for a drink after my shift. I said I'd tell them about something amazing they could do the next day. As soon as they left, the Armenian came over and, with a sneer, said, 'Michael, huh? No Will, no Wilfredo?' Somehow the word got out, because half an hour later Wilfredo Bonany himself turned up at the casino, hopping mad and accusing me of endangering his business. My name was Wilfredo. Was that so hard to remember? He was very sorry but I had to leave the job immediately. It turned out that the Armenian was from a similar organization, this time employing illegal immigrants from the Middle East, and his boss shared out the jobs with Bonany. So the Armenian mightn't have been Armenian but Iranian or Turkish or whatever. My slip had nearly wrecked the whole structure, and the best thing for me to do was to hightail it out of there. Make myself very scarce."

———

As I said, I've seen a lot of movies. I imagined Mike's descent into Sin City's circles of hell till he touched bottom all over again, but what he told me next was the exact opposite. In order to talk about his amorous adventures, he had to go back some months earlier. During his first week of parking cars, he left the motel and went looking for a room to rent. At the time, the United States was hit by a brutal recession, thanks to the housing bubble: Lehman Brothers, the risk premium, and the whole show. Sometimes, when he was riding a bus in streets on the outskirts of the city, Mike noticed that there were houses left unfinished, their gardens without lawns watched over by spindly palm trees, and frequently advertising rooms for rent. Many middle-class families in the stranglehold of crushing mortgage debts were struggling to earn a little extra cash on the side—money that wouldn't be directly snatched by the bank. One day Mike stopped at one of these houses and rang the doorbell. The family who lived there, a couple with a teenage son, was renting a furnished room.

"It was pretty basic," he said, "but it was air-conditioned and had a window looking out on the garden; and the best thing was that it had its own entrance, so I could come and go as I liked. It was at the back of the house and even had an en suite bathroom, although the brick walls had been left untiled. That was fine by me. When I showered, I felt like I was a fugitive half-hidden from the world. The deal also gave me the right to use the kitchen, of course. They kept a special shelf in the fridge for my things, and if I wanted to, I could warm up takeaways in the microwave oven or cook. In this regard, American families are much more open than we are and always willing to share everything. Yet, even so, I found it difficult to mix with them at first. I kept ungodly hours because of my parking shifts, and often when I got home at two in the morning they were asleep. At most, the light was on in the kid's room, where he was killing time with online video games. If I ran into them during the day, they always seemed frazzled or distant, as if they were ashamed of having a lodger in their house. I knew he was called Glenn and she was Jane and that they were more or less my age, but not much more than that. We agreed that I'd pay in cash every week, on Friday afternoon, and it was only in those few minutes that we exchanged the few platitudes permitted by my terrible English. They asked if I was happy and I sincerely thanked them, smiling and saying, 'OK, OK!'—which works for almost everything.

"When I'd been with them for three weeks and I had a Sunday off, I ran into Glenn and Jane at breakfast time. They offered me coffee and scrambled eggs and bacon, and that was how we broke the ice. As we ate, they asked about my job, the casino where I was working, and I told them as much as they could know. Then I asked what they did. Jane said she did nothing, that she was unemployed, and then she looked at her husband. 'I'm a loser,' Glenn said, rounding off his words with a bitter snigger."

It turns out that Glenn earned a living doing all kinds of odd jobs, under-the-counter stuff and shifty favors, all good for a few dollars, but what gave the family most financial stability was his job as a sparring partner in a gym where the brightest upcoming stars of Las Vegas boxing went to train. Years earlier, he himself had tried to make it as a welterweight but hadn't managed to go pro. However, his trainers could see that he was a great sparring partner, well able to take the punches, a decent guy who didn't take things personally. Some months before, as a result of the economic crisis, the insurance consultancy where he and Jane worked had gone bust, and all of a sudden the only alternative was to get back in the ring. This time he knew he'd always lose and he accepted that as part of the deal.

"I can't say I was shocked by this information," Mike Franquesa told me that afternoon, "because anything goes in Las Vegas, but, yes, after that I did see Glenn in a different light. From one day to the next he sprouted bulging muscles straining at his tracksuit. I looked at his knuckles and they gleamed like steel. His standoffishness made me think of someone who's always on the defensive, always waiting for the final fucking blow, if you pardon the expression. In any case, his presence didn't get threatening or involuntarily threatening—well, not for some months, at least. Not until Bonany gave me the sack. All at once, I was spending more time in the house, in my rented room, and inevitably Jane and I started fooling around when we were alone. Believe me, there's nothing easy about getting involved with a boxer's wife, however much of a loser he is; but love is blind, and there are things even the best intentions can't control. I'm telling you this as a former gambler."

I must have been looking incredulous at this twist in the story, or maybe Mike realized he was starting to sound mawkish, because he immediately wanted to clarify things. The morning after he was sacked, he got up feeling anxious and with no desire to talk. Thanks to his homesickness, he'd lost the only income he had in Las Vegas. He had some savings left but resisted working out how long they'd last. He knew from experience that the come-on of gambling, the lure of chips stacked on the table and money changing hands, was always lurking behind such reckonings, so he tried to ignore the temptation. That first morning, then, he automatically went out looking for work, doing the rounds of several casinos, offering himself as a valet parking attendant or anything else. He was willing to clean toilets if it came to that. But everywhere he went, they wanted references and documents, and he couldn't comply. That evening, seeing that he was at home at an hour when he was usually working, Glenn shyly knocked at his door to ask if he was all right.

"Can you imagine? I open up and there's this boxer with his nice-guy face asking how I am. The day before that he'd been KO'd at the gym, so he had a black eye and looked even more battered than I was. I told him I'd been kicked out because of a misunderstanding, but it was a temporary problem and I'd soon find something else. He tried to cheer me up, saying that they'd probably be quite happy to take me on at the gym as long as I didn't mind copping an inoffensive hammering from time to time. He offered to put in a word for me so I could become an apprentice sparring partner. (In other words, and let's be clear, this meant apprentice loser.) As tactfully as I could I said thanks, but no."

Mike Franquesa spent a few days feeling really down, even wondering if the time had come for him to return to Barcelona, but his survivor's instinct always won over frustration. He was fed up with watching television: too many channels, too many game shows that were no use at all for learning English, and this instinct of his told him he'd do better to use his time doing physical exercise and not brooding. One morning, moping round in the garden, he noticed that some tools had been dumped in one of the corners: a rake, a shovel, pruning shears that had started to rust . . . Without asking permission, he grabbed the hoe and got to work. The hot, dry climate didn't allow too much floral indulgence, but he still enjoyed transforming the wasteland he could see from his window.

"I remember that I'd been busting a gut for about an hour, trying to turn over that gritty ground, when I heard a door opening behind me and footsteps coming closer. I knew it was Jane and assumed she was going to tell me off for the liberty I'd taken. But when I turned, I saw she had a smile on her face and a hose in her hand. And she only wanted to tell me about the local government's water restrictions and the virtues of cactuses for decorating a desert landscape. That evening Glenn was nice about my prowess as a gardener while making it clear that my efforts wouldn't go toward paying for my room. 'Of course not,' I said. 'It's just to keep busy. And I'm getting experience along the way.'

"I worked in the garden early in the day, when the heat was bearable, and then went off to roam the city looking for work. Now I was adding to my résumé that I was an expert in gardening, landscaping, and even botany, but the days rolled by and I wasn't convincing anyone. Meanwhile, every morning Jane brought me a glass of lemonade and stayed for a chat as I worked in the garden. That's how we learned to look each other in the eye without embarrassment and exchange confidences, which, later on, when Glenn was there, we censored because of a kind of guilty sense of shame. When she went back inside, I imagined her sitting on the sofa, alone and lonely, looking for consolation in some novel by John Irving where, yeah, chance did change people's lives. In that microclimate, our storytelling gradually got bolder. An excessively hefty cactus made her laugh about Glenn's physical rigidity; a scrawny wild rhubarb plant reminded her of her nihilist adolescent son. I listened and laughed with a camaraderie that made her—and me, too—feel less alone. One day I asked if she'd let me search online for some botanical information about I forget which plant. She took me into the office and, under some pretext, showed me the whole house, the spaces that I'd had to imagine until then. Another day she asked me if I knew how to fix a tap. There was one in the kitchen that had been dripping for some days, and it was annoying her. She stayed at my side the whole time, watching me, and the kitchen was sparking with emotional electricity. We were both about to take the next step—you could feel it in the air—and if nothing happened then, it's because the scene was too cliché, like something out of a porn movie. The next day a comment about the bad luck dogging us both clinched the matter. Jane asked about my Zodiac sign and we had the same one: Sagittarius! What date was I born on? Incredibly we matched there. Year—

no, impossible—but that was the same too. Jackpot! We're the same age. We came into the world on exactly the same day, and in Las Vegas, coincidences involving numbers are always rewarded. We started our affair without complexes, relieved at last, convinced that destiny had decreed it, and that it would have been unforgivable sacrilege against the god of coincidence if we didn't."

Mike Franquesa got quite prolix at this point, maybe because he liked reliving the good moments of the relationship, but I won't record too many adulterous details now, except to say that the lovers enjoyed the thrill of lying and the natural highs and lows of it all for nearly four months. In the morning, as soon as Glenn went out the door, often tasked with taking their son to high school, Jane and Mike indulged in fantasies that were both romantic and methodical, a sped-up sex life that our hero recalled as self-conscious days of sheets and sloth, and other days of reckless risk-taking. When they fucked, Mike had to shoo away the image of Glenn coming through the door in his boxing gear, gloves dripping with blood and gore, about to give him a new face. Jane's imagination, in turn, transformed these gymnastic festivals into therapeutic exchanges, as if they, too, were a consequence of the financial crisis that had torpedoed their family life, justifying them with carpe diem, an expression she'd learned on some self-help website. Excitement did the rest, and Jane knocked at Mike's door with her heart racing a thousand miles an hour, a latter-day Lady Chatterley visiting the gamekeeper's hut.

"Now that I'm a long way from there and it's all in the

past, with no ill feelings for anyone," Mike said in the bar, "I'll tell you something that gives quite a good idea of how laid-back we were. One of the early days, when we'd been fucking all morning, I looked Jane in the eyes, hit my chest, and said, 'Me Tarzan, you Jane.' She laughed. It was a joke I'd been tempted to share from the beginning when she first told me her name, and now it seems to be a good summing-up of the jungle atmosphere, the almost zoolike logic of what we were getting up to."

"And how did her husband find out in the end? Don't tell me he caught you in flagrante . . ."

"No, no. Let's say we always managed to keep things well within the bounds of inscrutability. As I told you, in Las Vegas, apparently nothing can be normal. It's as if everything has to be sorted out on the fateful road to bankruptcy or, as in our case, with the clairvoyance that tells you when you have to stop playing. And it also turns out that sometimes two arbitrary but perfectly normal facts come together in one impossible combination. It's as simple as that. You don't know why, but all of a sudden a coincidence looks dubious. One day Jane went and got her hair cut short, a style she hadn't worn for years. That afternoon I drank one of Glenn's ginger beers. It was hot and I'd just finished my beers and was too lazy to go to the supermarket. He had a six-pack in the fridge. I thought he wouldn't mind and planned to replace it the next day. Glenn got back from the gymnasium, opened the fridge, and saw there was a bottle missing. Just then Jane came into the kitchen, sassy with her new hairdo, asking what he thought, and Glenn put two and two together. The mysterious arithmetic of coincidences. We'd been overconfident. At the time, he hid his feelings and praised Jane's hairdo—'You look so much younger!'—and didn't say a word about the ginger beer. That evening, though, she must have noticed that he was bemused, silent, distracted, as if he was weighing up the possibilities of adultery. At one point when I was alone with Jane, just the two of us in the kitchen, she looked at me wide-eyed, with raised eyebrows, without saying a word, and it wasn't difficult for me to decipher her message: *I think he suspects something.* The next morning everything seemed normal, but, just in case, I stayed out all day, pretending to be looking for work. I didn't see her, not for a single moment, and of course I missed her. That night I'd just got into bed, when there was a knock at the door. I stayed put. At first I thought it might be her, that Jane couldn't bear not seeing each other either, but then I was appalled by a terrible premonition. What if it was Glenn and he'd come to get even? The person knocked again, this time louder. I was ready for anything, and when I finally opened the door with my fists clenched and trembling all over, I was surprised to see the son. Now I realize I haven't even told you his name. It doesn't matter. The thing is, this kid, with his ganja-fogged brain and always in a trance, gave me instructions for my future. 'Leave tonight, please.' He told me this with all the aplomb of an older brother. 'You have to disappear. Tomorrow's Friday. Make it look as if you've cut and run because you can't pay the rent. My dad will forgive that, but another thing he won't. We've been having a hard time for years and we don't want to make things worse.' I took his advice and, a few hours later, scuttled away like a thief in the night."

"What about Jane?"

"I don't know anything about Jane. That's life. I kept convincing myself that we'd never really fallen in love, that the whole thing was just a way of not feeling lonely. But in fact, ever since then, I always think about her on our birthday and mentally send her a greeting."

Now working his way through his meal, Mike Franquesa went quiet again for a few seconds, observing some sort of reverential mourning rite for those superannuated times. Then, after calling the waiter to ask for another serving of french fries and more ketchup and mustard, he got on with his story. I watched him eating with a businesslike appetite without savoring the food, as if taking some kind of medicine. It was simply a matter of filling his stomach.

"So you see, after telling you all about my crazy love life, maybe I can now move on to my courtship with calories," he said smugly, tapping his prominent belly, "because, strange as it may seem, that's what saved my life and brought me to this point. After my nighttime escape, I went back to the Blue Cockatoo. It was a sort of return to origins. I felt as if I'd just arrived in Las Vegas, with everything to discover—although, with the experience of those months, I wasn't going to make the same errors. In a flash of lucidity, I understood that my future took me back to Wilfredo Bonany and, swallowing what pride I had left, I went looking for him in his usual haunts. Time heals all, I told myself, especially in a city where time has no value.

"Luckily, after the car parking fiasco, Wilfredo still valued my labor power and helped but also punished me. So, when he offered me a crappier, more demanding job, it also meant I earned more money. I was to be both dishwasher and diner in a restaurant. 'I assure you, you'll never be hungry,' he promised, trying to convince me to take it. The restaurant was near one of the most famous churches in Las Vegas, the Guardian Angel Cathedral, which mainly attracted penitents, the faithful needing to confess after nights of sex and alcohol, and loved-up brides and grooms who'd married in a fit of enthusiasm in a casino and now wanted to consolidate their conjugal status before God. It takes all kinds to make a world. The restaurant aimed to capture this pious clientele, and it was called the Loaves and the Fishes. And in case the gospels reference wasn't clear enough: its slogan was "All-You-Can-Eat Christian Buffet." The United States is full of crazies who believe these things and even more far-fetched stuff, and in this case, the singularity was that, as good Christians—but I don't know which particular branch, not to mention sect— the owners swore they threw nothing away. In other words, for a reasonable price, you walked out of there with a full belly and a clear conscience. Everything clients left on the plate, either because they were too full or didn't like the food, was eaten by us three dishwashers."

And that's how Mike Franquesa became a professional gorger. Besides washing dishes and pots and pans in the kitchen, he and his two colleagues took turns at sitting at a table in a corner of the restaurant, in front of everyone, acting out a particularly assertive kind of advertisement in which they polished off all the leftovers.

"When I started working there," he went on, "I was the beanpole and the other two dishwashers, who'd been there for a while, were the roly-polies. They took one look at me and started laughing. In five weeks I put on twenty kilos, believe me, and after that I stopped weighing myself. Since it was all-you-can-eat, the clients came and piled their plates high. The only condition was that, before taking the first bite, the head of the family had to say grace. Once the table and food were blessed, the Americans, who fortunately tend to enjoy life, didn't leave much, but there was always the stubborn brat who wouldn't open his mouth, or the wannabe model with eyes bigger than her belly, the kind who, with prodigious amounts of food stacked on her plate, suddenly gets finicky, takes a couple of mouthfuls, and complains she's full. After overcoming the revulsion of the first few days, I learned to eat without a second thought. Slices of bread and pizza with a sullen bite taken out of it just for show and fried rice and lasagna and guacamole and Caesar salad and corn on the cob and chunks of salmon and chicken wings and tiramisu . . . down it all went!"

Just listening to his list made me feel bloated and queasy, but Mike made it clear he didn't want me to interrupt.

"I have to say we chose it all in the kitchen, OK, and put it on clean plates. The owner was very scrupulous about these details because basically, for him, it was an article of faith. For example, we didn't have to strip bones that weren't chewed bare—no way—or lick up leftover grains of rice, or crumbs of fish, or streaks of sauce left on the plates. A limit was set and that limit was human dignity. At no point did we feel like rats in a garbage dump, or even hobos in a soup kitchen, but just that we were getting paid to stuff ourselves.

"What did bother us, if anything, were the cooks. There was an Indian who used too much spice and chili, and a half-French guy who put cream in all the sauces. With this diet dictated by the daily whims of cooks and clients, our digestive systems were in a terrible state and we were antacid junkies. In the long run, of course, this deal changed your character. I got a decent wage, and I had a full belly and quite a lot of free time, but the days were getting more and more boring. Insipid as a plate of boiled rice. So one night, after leaving work, I went into a casino gaming room again and, this time, with my wallet more or less full of dollars."

"I guess that was inevitable," I ventured. "But I still don't understand how you detoxed. Or have you been stringing me along all this time and now you're going to ask me for money?"

"Don't offend me," he said, brandishing a french fry at me, smiling as he dunked it in ketchup and put it in his mouth, savoring the pleasure of telling me his story. "I remember that the casino was the Paris Las Vegas, and as you can imagine, that night I threw myself into the arms of the goddess Fortune and soon lost every cent I had on me. A week's pay. Six days of washing plates and pots and pans and, moreover, downing kilos of chicken curry. (At the time, the Indian cook had just returned from a trip back home and was battling his homesickness with chili.) To make matters worse, the casinos in Las Vegas, never losing sight of the point of the game, set the betting limit much higher than it is in Barcelona, which means you win or lose faster. When I saw that I didn't have a single dollar left, I started retching and went outside to puke in the street, under an ornamental palm tree. I felt empty like I hadn't felt for months, but, needless to say, it wasn't a nice emptiness. I looked up, took in the whole scene around me, and, for the first time since I arrived, I felt like a jerk, a bum, a total louse. They should have given me a part in the musical they were doing in that nearby theater. Like so many others hanging around the sidewalks of the city, I'd joined the army of specters floating about, lost at all hours of the day and night, always on the lookout for one last dollar to stake, always waiting for the chance to snatch a few more hours of hope. Wanderers consumed by debt; lives run aground in a bog of sand and make-believe; the unemployed, the pensioners, the unskilled youths, losers of every color and ethnic group who'd been chasing a dream for a long time, and now they only wanted to connect with reality by way of roulette, cards, or a jackpot. You could see them leaving the pawnshops, sagging invertebrates in tracksuits, shambling away after receiving a pittance for a watch, a set of barbells, a plastic-covered autograph signed years ago by Cher . . .

"Realizing that I was one of them, my first reaction was

to put an end to it all. That was easy. I only had to climb up the Eiffel Tower at the casino, which was nearly as high as the original one, and throw myself off it. A vaguely romantic suicide, product of imitation, though the death would have been real."

Instead of opting for such a tragicomic fate, Mike made a decision that looks terrible at first sight but, in the end, it saved his life. In other words, he went looking for a way of "financing" his gambling habit.

"This needs some explaining," he noted. "One of the things I learned parking cars was that nobody gets dressed up in Las Vegas except for workers. Uniforms are a trademark distinguishing between workers and bosses, between customers and the guys who keep the show going, and I'd gotten into the habit of wearing well-ironed trousers and a matching jacket. This was indirect advice from the tight-lipped Armenian who once opened his mouth to observe that uniforms attract tips. And it was true. That night of my relapse, I stood by one of the entrances, pretending I was superintending the parking operation, and it didn't take me long to get a tip. And then another. Very soon, thanks to the benevolence of a few generous clients, I had a hundred bucks, the minimum bet for most of the tables. Then I took off my jacket, went into the casino, changed my money for chips, and started to play . . ."

"So let *me* tell the story now: you won." I made a dramatic pause for him to fill with a laugh, but Mike looked daggers at me. "No. You lost again."

"Exactly. They cleaned me out once more. But, anyhow,

that's not the important part. What happened is that, after losing the whole lot in ten minutes, like a total greenhorn, I couldn't react. In the claws of the chimera I stared at the roulette ball, the green velvet, numbers, chips, hands sweeping up and down. I think of it now and tell myself it was pretty well the same as being in Barcelona that summer of the final rout, as if not a single day had gone by. Then I started watching a player who was sitting at the head of one of the tables, a fair-haired, athletic, cocky peacock of a guy escorted by three spectacular girls who clapped their hands and tittered every time he won. The chips he was raking in were piling up in front of him like buildings in a gorgeous multicolored little city, and I was suddenly swamped with envy. I took a dislike to the guy. I know it was arbitrary. But then, almost immediately, he started losing. And losing. In no time at all he'd lost the lot and, watching him deflate, I revived inside. I even felt hungry. When the peacock got up and left with the three wilting chicks halfheartedly straggling after him, I went over to another table. A Chinese couple was sitting there in silence and playing punctiliously, as if they were discussing each bet following an extended telepathic calculation. Their winnings also had me drooling, and the more I concentrated on their formal, almost ritual gestures, the more they lost. I cleaned them out, in a manner of speaking, and the same thing happened at two other tables. I wasn't winning but I was making other people lose. Then a security guy came over and asked me to accompany him. 'What have I done?' I asked, but he didn't answer. He took me to an even better dressed gentleman who said, 'We've been watching you from our control room. You, sir, are a cooler.' I didn't get it, so I asked him to explain. 'You, sir, have an extremely rare gift. Your aura of mediocrity breaks the best winning streaks and the luckiest clients start losing systematically. You have to work for us.'"

Later, I discovered that in the parlance of the Valencia region, this kind of bearer of misfortune in casinos and card games is called a *cremaor*. In other words, guys like Mike Franquesa cool the game in Las Vegas but in Valencia they burn it, but both coolers and burners steer players away from the road to Lady Luck. The day after this revelation Mike Franquesa stopped being a dishwasher and professional guzzler and started working in the casino as a cooler. In any case, he didn't stop frequenting the Christian all-you-can-eat, not because he was one of the faithful but because he understood that his ability to mess with the luck of others was linked with leading the good life himself. If he lost a little weight, he was less effective. As I said, he told me this story one summer afternoon, stuffing himself all the while, getting ready for his shift at the Barcelona casino.

"I must be the first professional cooler in Catalonia," he said with undisguised pride. "Sooner or later, we all get to find out what role we have to play in the theater of life."

PATIENCE

I was in a café at the Luxembourg railway station and had just finished a sandwich and a Coca-Cola. I asked for the bill and wanted to pay by credit card. The waiter brought the terminal and asked me to key in my PIN. Meanwhile, for a few seconds, he stared into the distance, at some indeterminate point. All salespeople and waiters do this. They look at nothing, being discreet and offering a little privacy to the client. Some don't make much effort to pretend and turn their faces away looking put out or overcome with an attack of shyness, but there are others who go into personal daydream mode, closing their eyes for a few seconds to look at an imaginary horizon and not coming back to the real world until the machine makes some kind of sound. Maybe we should give a name to this brief, vague, mental vanishing point. Maybe we should call it Timbuktu or Farawayland . . . Well, anyway, I keyed in my number while the Luxembourger waiter got lost in his vanishing point somewhere in the south, toward Marseille or further down, wherever, and the little screen showed some words in French: *Veuillez patienter.* I wondered how we could translate that. The most logical rendering would be "Wait a moment, please" or something similar, but in fact what interested me was the verb *patienter.* I don't think we have an equivalent verb in Catalan but only the opposite, *impacientar,* and the derivative *despacientar.* Yet, if the screens on our machines said, "Wait a moment. Don't get impatient," we'd take it as a slight, as if we were jittery to begin with, or testy because the whole thing was too slow and wasting time. I understand that, for the French, the *Veuillez patienter* is gentler. It's just an idiom you don't take to heart, and maybe you don't even read it. All right, then, I'll wait for a few seconds. You're welcome.

———

All this stuff was running round my head while I was on the platform waiting for the train. I was going to Nancy to take part in a literary game, which was actually a commission. It was the strangest proposition I'd ever been offered as a writer, or the second strangest, perhaps. The idea was I had to go to have dinner in the house of some people I don't know, together with other guests, and then write something about the experience or the conversations that came up during the evening. They weren't strangers chosen haphazardly. No, it wasn't as if you just rang at any old door and announced you were going there for dinner. The organizers had taken care in selecting as hosts people who liked talking, listening, and discussing, who were interested in literature, and who, in turn, could tell me things about Nancy or whatever else they felt like.

Apart from the mystery of going into the house of strangers and sharing several hours with them, knowing I'd probably never see them again unless something unexpected happens to change our lives—which tends not to be the case—what most intrigued me was how all this might be filtered into a story. As I understand it, there are two kinds of narrators: hunters and fishers. Hunters go out to get the literary material, setting off into unknown territories with all their senses on the alert to find a story, a character, a thread to tug at, or revelation that will open up the way of the word, almost like medieval knights getting into their armor, mounting their steeds, and riding off into adventure. Then there are the fisher narrators who sit on the riverbank and cast a line. They're still and patient, quietly waiting for the fish to take the bait. If the story doesn't come their way, they ponder life and fill the waiting time with imagination and thoughts, and at the end of the day it might happen that what they've actually caught is more or less an excuse to describe everything that's been swimming around in their heads.

I can't say what kind of narrator I am. Sometimes I'm a kind of axman striding out to hunt and other times, perhaps more often, I just stay still and try to fish. I was thinking all this on the train and, in fact, I realized that, right

then, I was doing both things at once: I was going somewhere looking for a story and at the same time I was sitting still looking at the scenery. What I could see through
the window was fairly monotonous anyway. Green plains
of central Europe, newly harvested fields, deep, wide riv-
ers, and, in the distance, forests and bell towers steeped
in the colors of afternoon sunlight. Sometimes the train
stopped at a medium-size town—Bettembourg, Thionville,
Hagondange—and now, about an hour into the journey, we
were coming into Metz. We left behind an industrial park
and slowly entered the city center, and if I'm talking about
this, it's because I noticed a stretch of tents and shacks
made of cardboard and cloth. A miniature city improvised
inside another city. You could see movement there, especially women working at something or sitting in groups.
It seemed that they'd settled in the parking lot behind a
shopping mall and next to a loading dock.

"Refugees," someone in the compartment said. He
must have seen me looking intently through the window
and was almost answering my thoughts. "A few months
ago the police broke up this camp, but they've been coming
back in dribs and drabs."

"Are they Syrians?" I asked.

"No, as far as I know, most of them are Albanians and
Kosovars. They come through the Baltic countries. They
want documents, of course, and they're waiting. Weeks and
weeks until the government can find somewhere to house
them. They're counting on a solution by the fall, before the
cold sets in."

I wanted to ask him about the city hall and public opinion, but we pulled into the Metz railway station. I had to change trains and lost sight of my informant. Ten minutes later I was settled in another compartment. The car was quite full, and as we pulled out of the station, two young women came in and sat down. They were about twenty, trendily dressed in tight jeans and designer blouses. The one sitting opposite me took a makeup kit from her handbag. Her expression was glassy and her eyes swollen from crying.

"Did you lock the door?" she asked her friend. She said it in French but I picked up a strong accent. She was probably American.

"No," said the other one. "You had the keys, didn't you?"

They both laughed. They were sharing a bottle of orange juice, which they passed back and forth. The one opposite me patted her pockets and confirmed that, yes, she did have the keys. Then they went on with the conversation. Neither of them was convinced that the door had been locked. I understood that with all the rush and excitement of getting away they'd probably forgotten about it.

"Well, I left my suitcase and bags in the entrance," said the worrier, now busy redoing her eye shadow. "If people see it's not locked, they only have to take three steps and grab the lot. It's that easy."

"No, it's not that easy. From outside, the door looks locked," said her friend, trying to reassure her. Then she changed the subject. "So, anyway, how did he react? Tell me again."

"Nothing to tell. He said he'll come and see me in Cleveland in the summer, but I know he won't. They say these things and then they don't happen. When he saw I was starting to cry, though . . ." She fell silent for a moment. "I think we have to go back. It's too risky."

Her friend, who was sitting next to me, huffed in exasperation. "But what about Nancy? When can we go?"

"We've still got time. We'll go home, lock the door properly, and get the next train. We'll only lose an hour."

"I think you did lock the door. We'll be going all the way back for nothing. And we'll be really annoyed when we get there and see that it was locked all the time! You only have a few hours left in France, and this is how you go and waste them . . ."

They went on arguing for another ten minutes, until we got to the next station, where they got out. They didn't say goodbye to me. Didn't say anything. I might as well not have been there. I couldn't work out what they were going to do in Nancy either, whether it was important or not. For a few moments I thought there was another boyfriend involved, and some money, and I must confess I was about to intervene in the conversation and ask what was going on. If I'd done that, I would have become a hunter-writer, then and there, but I think I desisted, because the time wasn't right yet. I hadn't even got to Nancy and didn't want to seem like a predator, a guy desperate to grab a good story, and the sooner the better. When the train started moving again, I watched them walking along the platform. The woman from Cleveland was carrying the bottle of orange juice in her hand. She saw me at the window and our eyes met for a few seconds. She stopped in her tracks as if she remembered something and made a grimace of surprise, which was frozen by the movement of the train. Then I couldn't see her anymore. Forgotten on the seat opposite me lay her makeup kit.

———

The makeup kit is here in front of me as I write these words. I kept it. A useless trophy. It's a long, narrow case containing everything you'd expect to find. Eye shadow, face powder, and even a little mirror. I take out the lipstick, ketchup red, and open it. Now I could say that I'm putting it on my lips, and I like it, like myself, and the little mirror reflects my mouth, so I pout at it, thinking this isn't me, that I'm another biography, even that of the jumpy, teary American woman. Or that, when the train got to Nancy, I discovered that, inside the makeup case, there was a card with a phone number, which I called and it was a striptease club, or that there was a photo of the woman with some guy, or even an engagement ring that looked more like costume jewelry . . . All at once I can see a whole slew of possibilities, and there'd even be more if I added the refugees I saw from the train coming into Metz. After all, they lived in the same city as that young woman, passing through like she was, with their whole lives packed into bits of luggage . . . But then I tell myself to calm down.

When I got to the hotel in Nancy, I went up to my room and unpacked my bag. The atmosphere, the ritual, and the movements we all make when we go into a hotel room made me feel like someone who is used to this nomadic life, like a traveling salesman. It dawned on me that maybe that was what they wanted from me, to be a peddler of stories, except I was going there to buy and not to sell. In an attempt to combat this uncomfortable sensation, I put the few clothes I'd brought in the wardrobe and left a couple of books and a folder on the desk, trying to give the room some personality. I needed to inhabit it. I went to the toilet and then stretched out on the bed to test the quality of the mattress and especially the softness of the pillows. I always do that.

Lying there, with his eyes closing, the man recalled a passage from Fernando Pessoa's *Book of Disquiet*: "Only those who don't seek are happy, because only those who don't seek find." Therefore, it was about not looking for anything, and when he woke up from his late siesta, he went out into the street in that spirit. It was six in the afternoon in Nancy and the sun was setting.

That evening he had no dinner commitment and, with the same ease with which a narrator can switch from first to third person, started walking in the city. In the portfolio the organizers had left for him at the hotel, there was a map of Nancy. He looked at it for a moment and decided to head west, toward the old quarter. Then he put it in his jacket pocket.

A few days earlier, in Barcelona, a French friend had told him about the discreet beauty of Nancy and how art nouveau façades appeared in the most surprising places.

She told him not to miss the potent splendor of Place Stanislas, with its golden gateways, centuries-old cobblestones, and inviting terrace bars full of people. However, he deliberately avoided it. When he saw that the end of the street opened into a wide square and heard the murmur of voices, he went off in a different direction. Since he hadn't been given the address, he kept toying with the idea that one of those houses might be where he was going to end up the next day, having dinner with a bunch of strangers. He could go to any door and ring the bell, pretending he'd got the day wrong. Then the more-than-stranger strangers, which is to say people who'd never as much as thought about meeting him, would tell him that he hadn't gotten the day wrong but the place, because they weren't expecting anyone, or maybe they'd let him in, but most probably they'd coolly bid him goodbye, because who knows what he might have interrupted.

These imagined scenes appealed to him and mortified him in equal measure. He couldn't avoid indulging, and yet he felt tainted, as if he were cheating. The exercise of being a non-searcher was leading to total inertia, but if that was the case, it would have been better to stay in his hotel room and watch the news on television. After half an hour of aimless walking he came to a square with a fountain and an equestrian statue in the middle. It was an unassuming square, perhaps because it lay in the intimidating shadow of a neo-Gothic church, and it had a strange name: Place Saint-Épvre. Here, too, there were three or four terrace bars, but they were a little untidy looking and their clients seemed to be regulars, local residents. He sat down outside a brasserie and asked for a flask of wine and a serving of quiche Lorraine with salad. From where he was sitting he could see a patisserie with the usual bustle of that hour on a Friday afternoon, a closed travel agency, and a woman who was in the process of closing her flower stall. Next to him, a gentleman was enjoying a beer and reading *L'Est Républicain* but also looking up occasionally to greet people walking by. He did this with practiced elegance, as if the corner of his eye was more attentive to them than to his newspaper.

It all had an everyday air, and from his table he admiringly took in the whole scene. In tranquil harmony, cars, passersby, and pigeons were all getting on with things as if on a movie set, and he almost expected a director somewhere in the wings to call out, "Action!" He took a sip of wine, diligently savoring it as if by acting, too, he could get this sham idea out of his head.

In a way that was very natural, he went back to Place Saint-Épvre a few more times during his stay in Nancy. He even sat in the same chair twice. Although he went at different times of the day, he was looking for the feeling of repetitive routine. He wanted the waiters to recognize him, and on the last day his intimate victory was when the man reading *L'Est Républicain* looked up and greeted him with a nod as he approached on the sidewalk.

———

The next day he got up in a different mood. When you wake up after spending a night in a new city, you feel as if it's more yours. Since he had the whole day free—his appointment for dinner with the strangers wasn't until seven that evening—he kept strolling around Nancy without a map. He'd cross the bridge over the railway line, head toward the riverside walk, and go into the cathedral. Random wandering would be his way of relating with the city, stitching it together in little bits as if a detective were following him and it was necessary to make him understand that he wasn't looking for anything. He mentally shied away from the word "serendipity."

Having breakfast in the hotel dining room, he overheard a conversation at a nearby table: two young women talking about literature, the novels they'd read recently, and a woman writer they couldn't stand. All of a sudden there was a crash. At another table a man had fallen to the ground when he was going to sit down. In fact, the chair had broken. Its design was too flimsy for his weight. He went to help the man up and retrieved from the floor two small paperbacks and a sheaf of crumpled papers. He peeked at the content: notes for a talk on the work of Marie Darrieussecq. Later on, in the street, this sensation of a literary plot only intensified. Two young guys standing at some traffic lights were discussing the relevance of symbolist poetry today. When he reached the Excelsior brasserie, he thought he saw James Ellroy—recognizable because of his Hawaiian print shirt—who was crossing the street, looking dejected, and as if he was running away from someone. When he walked past the L'Autre Rive bookshop he saw that it was jam-packed and, at the very back, a young woman was reading aloud to the crowd. These coincidences kept happening over and over again, all morning. He took refuge in a café and found that the waiter spoke in Alexandrine verse, like a Victor Hugo in modern-day Lorraine. This was the world turned topsy-turvy, a conspiracy aimed at getting him to stop his aimless drifting, and it forced him to remember that he wasn't desperate and wasn't looking for anything.

Walking where his feet took him and blindsided by this surfeit of literary signals, he inadvertently came to Place Stanislas. Then he understood everything. At one end of the lordly expanse, some panels announced that there was a major literary festival in Nancy that weekend. "More than two hundred guest writers," one pennant proclaimed. People were queuing at the entrances of buildings to hear their favorite authors, buy books, and ask for an autograph.

Faced with this scene, the first reaction of Felipe Quero—now it's time to give him a name—was to turn tail and vanish. He'd certainly feel like a traveling salesman there! Moreover, the milieu wasn't in the least inspiring. He couldn't stand fiction about writers. As a reader, he felt it was far removed from reality, anecdotal, and smug. As an author, if he tried to write about the small talk and squabbles of the people in his trade, he felt false and naked.

The discovery opened up a crack in his self-esteem. Sure, a literary festival . . . but how come the organizers hadn't even mentioned it? This jab at his pride put him on his guard. His name didn't appear among those of the two hundred guest writers, which quickly led to a premonition. What if the dinner was a pretext to make fun of him? The

French are capable of cooking up that kind of trick . . .
Maybe the invitation concealed a trap that would turn him
into literary fodder, a joke in bad taste. Now he had to be
vigilant.

Perturbed and aggrieved, he was thinking about all
this as he was walking away, but at the same time, with
each step he took, he was increasingly aware of a physical lightness that was unusual for him. He wasn't carrying
a briefcase or anything cumbersome and, happily sticking
his hands in his pockets, he realized that, in this particular
vanity fair, nothing about him would give him away as a
fiction writer. He could move around totally incognito. So
he went into one of the tents and strolled past the book
stalls. It was full of people. Behind their tables, writers were
waiting for readers to come and ask for a signature. A lot
of them looked bored but, managing to stay patient, were
covering up their jadedness by flipping through the pages of
some book or another by the publisher concerned (although
an hour later they wouldn't even recall the title).

Felipe Quero observed them indifferently, like someone on the other side of the looking glass, and this double-
agent mode made him feel more confident. When he tired
of staring at writers, he went off to the other end of the
fair, near the Parc de la Pépinière, and entered a street that,
he worked out, should take him to Place Saint-Épvre. At
some point, however, he changed course, because he was
now walking toward one of the city's medieval gateways,
the Porte de la Craffe. He crossed over to admire its majes-
tic, ominous presence and, once on the other side of the

road, noticed a rather odd couple, a man and a woman, well into their sixties—pensioners, perhaps. The woman was looking at the gateway and he was taking her photo. Felipe Quero saw that the setup was strange. The man didn't seem at all interested in the two towers and the whole massive defensive structure but, rather, in his wife looking at the complex, as if the Porte de la Craffe was only worthy of attention when she was observing it, and precisely because she was observing it. Felipe moved away from the scene and walked down the main street, where shops along both sides were offering all sorts of tourist enticements. Not long afterwards, he ran into the couple again. Now the woman was admiring the Palace of the Dukes of Lorraine, its white façade and Gothic-style balconies, and her man was immortalizing her in the act of contemplating the monument. On this second occasion he noticed that she was well aware of being photographed and was adopting a certain pose. The connection between them seemed to be a desire to play or to act something out. Their performance looked affected and even perverse, and for the first time since he'd arrived in Nancy, Felipe thought that it might be worth pulling at that narrative thread. He watched them from a discreet distance, wondering whether to follow them or not, but the couple disappeared into a patisserie, and he took this as a sign to leave them to it.

A few meters farther on he saw Place Saint-Épvre and, wanting to rest for a while, went to sit in the same terrace bar as the previous day. Drinking his Perrier, he told himself to be more patient, a little cooler in exploring the mystery of the roaming couple, and as he was thinking this, they turned up in his field of vision yet again. He watched her stop by the equestrian stature of René II, Duke of Lorraine, staring at it with excessive interest while her husband took a couple of photos. This comedy went on for a while, enough time for Felipe to get out his cell phone and take a photo of them without their noticing.

————

At half past six that evening, as arranged with the organizers, a taxi came to get him at the hotel and take him to the dinner. As they drove through the streets and around the traffic circles of Nancy, heading for a less central neighborhood, Felipe Quero looked at the photo he'd taken that midday. The slightly skewed angle gave it a furtive feel, like a spy game, highlighting the couple's weird behavior, although their faces remained half-hidden. He tried enlarging the image on the screen but didn't find anything of note. The woman was looking sideways, and the man was semiconcealed by the arm holding the camera. With these two ill-defined physiognomies, he told himself, the couple had all they needed to become fiction. It was easy to take the next step and speculate that, at the dinner, there'd probably be a couple who fitted the same profile.

Thus it was that his mission began in practice the moment his hosts welcomed him and he thanked them for their invitation. All in all, they told him, there'd be ten people present that night. It turned out that his hosts were from Morocco: pleasant, attentive people whose warmth made him feel at home. He, Karim, was a chef at his own restaurant. That night he'd cooked a Moroccan meal. Chaymae, his partner, was a lecturer in philosophy at the college. Bright-eyed and with an engaging smile, she told Felipe that she'd read his last novel and liked it a lot, which puffed up his ego for the rest of the evening. They took him out into the garden where the appetizer was being served and introduced him to their friends, the other guests. There was a librarian, a Tunisian musician who played the oud—a kind of lute played in the Arab world; a lawyer and a sociologist, both very discreet and apparently good friends; and a couple whom Felipe Quero instantly imagined could represent his two strangers. They were middle-aged and slightly standoffish. She painted realist portraits but in dirty style—there was one of Chaymae hanging in the living room—and he was an art critic specializing in forgeries.

While chatting with this couple, trying to work out how well they fitted with the morning's photographer and his model, he mentally counted the guests. Nine. Then someone rang the bell and Chaymae went to open the door. The tenth person was another writer, a Catalan called Jordi Puntí, and Felipe Quero stared at him in some consternation. He knew the man by name but hadn't read his books, and in these early moments Puntí seemed to be a little too grateful to his hosts, almost smarmy. Felipe had been more restrained, even a little distant, and now the contrast made him feel bad. He heard Chaymae telling Puntí that she'd read his last novel in translation and the coincidence made him seethe with inner fury. Was it his imagination or was Chaymae sounding more enthusiastic this time? He started fretting all over again: maybe he was a sort of fairground dummy after all, a secondary character at the service of this other writer . . . He went over to Puntí, greeted him, and none too subtly asked how come he was there. Then everything became clear. Some months earlier, Puntí had met the art critic in Hamburg at some cultural gathering and they'd become friends. Now, since he was taking part in the Nancy literary festival that weekend, they'd invited him to the dinner.

"They told me that you're the guest of honor and that all this is part of some literary project," Puntí said. "Good for you! I couldn't do it."

"Why?"

"I find it very difficult to write commissioned pieces. I'd get flustered. I tend to be all over the place. Do you know what you're going to write about?"

"I've got some ideas . . ." Felipe Quero prolonged the uncertainty by letting it trail off into ellipsis.

The conversation relaxed. In the first few minutes he'd understood that the other guests saw him as a home-delivery storyteller, someone who was going to brighten their evening. Since they were in France, he automatically saw himself as being in a kind of nineteenth-century literary salon, complete with frock coat and pipe, and proffering very emphatic or very sibylline opinions, but then he reminded himself that he'd come to this dinner mainly to listen. If something came out of this gathering, if he managed to hunt or fish some item, time would tell. On further consideration, even the photo-taking couple was becoming an anecdote, a background story that maybe—and this was yet to be decided—wouldn't go much beyond that.

By the time they were seated at the table, this receptive position was more palpable. The food was delicious and the red wine relaxed the formality. Karim had made fish soup and then chicken tagine with prunes and dates. The flavors, both intense and refined, led them to talk about the Mediterranean connection, the hedonist lifestyle that the inhabitants of western Europe tasted only when they went south on vacation. The Tunisian musician talked about the melodies that traveled around the Mediterranean in folk music or traditional songs as a nexus of cultural unity, while Karim drove the point home by referring to Andalusi nubah. "It's the music of patience," he said, and Felipe looked up from his plate.

Karim and the musician began to explain that nubah originated in the Maghreb states of North Africa and were influenced by flamenco and the culture of Andalusia. According to the tradition, there were initially twenty-four original compositions, or nubat, one for each hour of the day and lasting exactly sixty minutes, so that the whole cycle lasts twenty-four hours. They are played with several percussion and string instruments like the oud and are accompanied by a chorus. Nowadays, it's almost impossible to hear a complete cycle, but they still do sessions of nine or ten hours, which audiences, swept up in the ebb and flow of the experience, follow without losing interest.

"It's music that grows inside you as you listen," the Tunisian musician said, "constantly progressing in keeping with the rules of quickening rhythm that change from region to region. Later on, I can play a sample for you . . ."

They all accepted the offer, and over mint tea and dessert—pistachio pastries and sweet eggplant—the conversation broke up into small groups. At his end of the table, Felipe Quero, tuning in to them all, heard the librarian make a comment about Hannah Arendt, the lawyer talking about the tomatoes sold in French markets, the art critic from Hamburg describing the feats of one of Germany's main forgers, a man named Wolfgang Beltracchi, and the lawyer quizzing Puntí about the political situation in Catalonia, a conversation joined by the Tunisian musician, who added his bit by commenting that the national anthem of Spain was brazenly copied from a twelfth-century Andalusi nubah. There was prodigious abundance in these intense shifts of stories and conversations that captivated Felipe Quero in a way not unlike images of a shoal of salmon struggling to swim upstream, rising from the water in surprising leaps against the current. He wished he had eight ears.

After a while, Chaymae suggested that they should go and sit on the sofas. The musician took this as his cue and got ready to play and sing, occasionally accompanied by Chaymae's voice. To begin with, he chose ancient Arab songs, compositions that swaddled them in repetition while transporting them back to other times. He set to music classical forms like zajals and kharjas and then gradually ventured into modern poets like Victor Hugo, Apollinaire, and García Lorca, and finally he played his own compositions. Felipe Quero watched how passionately the man lived his music, how his face became transfigured with it, and there were moments when he felt impatient. This guy was so keen to show them different kinds of music and to try out his new compositions, and it was all dragging on too long. Then, after they'd been listening for about an hour, he announced a song inspired by an Andalusi poet. He played the first chords, recited the first lines, and then, prodded by some kind of haste, stopped and abruptly announced, "Et cetera."

It was an extraordinary moment, a startling departure from the script, and everyone started to laugh. Then there was a silence that, while not intending to be accusatory, was precisely that. The sociologist—who, up to that point, had been very quiet—filled it by praising the music. "I think it's very inspiring," he said. "There's deep interplay in the combination of notes which makes it more contemplative. I don't want to come on as a mystic, but there's very powerful evocative strength here even when you're not sure what you want to evoke." The musician couldn't resist accompanying his words with four or five bars. "Some of you already know that in my free time I do hypnotism, that I'm a therapeutic hypnotist. When I was listening to the music a moment ago, I had the feeling that all those melodies were dragging me into the world of the unconscious . . ."

These comments made a great impression on the other guests. Felipe Quero wasn't sure if it was a teasing joke but then saw that everyone else was taking it very seriously. They started asking the sociologist about hypnosis and he responded with professional devotion. He made it clear that this wasn't a business or a show seeking to ridicule people but an exercise in deferred psychological self-control that could be very useful. Then Karim asked the question they all had on the tips of their tongues: "And could you give us a demonstration tonight?"

"I don't think it would work," the sociologist replied. "There are too many people. It's better when it's done in private, just the two of us . . . But, anyhow, if you want, we can try. Only so you can get an idea of what's involved, without being able to go into it too deeply."

Karim volunteered. Chaymae turned off the lights and only a few candles on the coffee table were left burning. The light bounced off wineglasses, the atmosphere became more intimate, and Karim lay on the sofa. Beside him, the hypnotist took a pendulum from his pocket and, staring at it, intent but not tense, pronounced some relaxing words. Sitting around him but at a certain distance, the rest were breathing in synchrony . . .

But it didn't work. After a minute Karim stood up and said they should leave it. He'd drunk too much and couldn't concentrate. There was a murmur of disappointment and the hypnotist said not to worry. It wasn't unusual.

Felipe Quero wondered for a few seconds whether he should volunteer for this hypnosis session. This might be the moment he was waiting for, the engine of a story which would surge from his subconscious, in front of everyone.

Then, however, Jordi Puntí beat him to it and, taking advantage of the lull in the conversation, said that if the other guests didn't mind, he'd like to try, too. From his corner, Felipe Quero mutely cursed him with all his might and glanced at the other guests almost as if trying to infect them with his annoyance. After all, wasn't he the guest of honor? No one seemed to notice. The sociologist was happy to comply and asked Puntí to get comfortable on the sofa.

This time the hypnotist's chant was clearer and Puntí let himself go. It was evident that he was a willing subject. His arms and legs looked lifeless and his belly rose and fell in time with the leisurely rhythm of his breathing. Concentrating on the pendulum, it seemed to him that he was going down a very long staircase, with narrow steps and no handrail, slowly taking him to swampy ground with low mists and squelchy mud. As his eyes closed, he gazed into the distance, a vanishing point that could be Timbuktu or Farawayland. It was a place that both tempted and frightened him, but, with its outlines now being defined, a voice coming from outside him was telling him that he couldn't stop. When he got to the bottom, he didn't know whether three minutes, three days, or three years had gone by.

Author's Note

All the stories in this volume have already had a dress
rehearsal in the form of publication in some other place:
magazines, newspapers, or jointly authored volumes . . .
All of them, too, were commissioned and briefly presented,
after which they went off to sleep the sleep of the just. The
oldest among them are seventeen years old and are con-
temporaries of the stories in the collection *Animals tris-
tos* (Empúries, 2002). The more recent ones were written
in 2016. Although the initial impulse was almost always
external, I wrote them with the same literary rigor as I
would any other story. If there was some prior stipulation—
regarding characters, theme, and setting—I molded it to fit
the style I wanted. That's why now, some time later, they
have probably earned the right to appear in this collection.

One of the more usual problems of commissioned works

is length. It almost always affects me, more on the side of excess than brevity, and I frequently have to cut what I've written in order to deliver the final text. Now, totally free and with a touch of revenge, I've recovered some of those excluded fragments. I've also taken the opportunity to rewrite some of the stories, especially the older ones, in the hope of making them more amenable to today's readers. In the process, I've discovered that, however much you rewrite a text or want to rid it of temporal ingenuousness, there are things that never disappear: the hallmark of the moment when you wrote it, the person you were, the literary concerns that moved you, and even the world around you. For example, one of the stories, "Consolation Prize," is now subtitled "An Analogical Tale" because nowadays, in the era of cell phones, the Internet, and social networks, Ibon's adventures would have taken another route. In fact, the whole thing would be so predictable, it wouldn't even be worth writing about.

Reading and revising these stories, I picked up a coincidence I hadn't foreseen: music plays a prominent role and is not always merely decorative or atmospheric. I guess that's inevitable. I mean that the general bent of the book reveals my musical curiosity. Hence, while I was working on this collection, it seemed to me that the title had to reflect this constant presence, which is why I decided on *This Is Not America*. Written and recorded by David Bowie and Pat Metheny, "This Is Not America" is a song I like because of the calm it conveys, and also because they expressly composed it as a soundtrack for the movie *The Falcon and the*

Snowman. Moreover, as a natural consequence of this musical affiliation, I find echoing in the spirit of some of the stories lines of a poem written by Enric Casasses and set to music by Pascal Comelade. Titled "Amèrica," it begins with the words which I have made mine: *"Amèrica és el poble del costat"* ("America's the next village").

In recognition of the first life of these nine stories, I shall now offer in chronological order some details about their original appearance.

An early version of "Consolation Prize: An Analogical Tale" appeared with the title "Com si demanés un desig" ("As if He Made a Wish") in the collection of love stories *Tocats d'amor* (Columna, 2000) by the Germans Miranda collective.

A first version of "My Best Friend's Mother" ("La mare del meu millor amic") appeared in *La vida sexual dels germans M.* by the Germans Miranda collective (Columna, 2002), an anthology of erotic stories.

"Seven Days on the Love Boat" ("Set dies al Vaixell de l'Amor") was commissioned by the Saló Nàutic (International Boat Show) of Barcelona and was published in a Catalan-Spanish bilingual edition with drawings by Mariscal (Mòbil Books, 2006).

"Matter" ("La matèria") was first published only in Spanish translation with the title "Veo veo Mr. Materia" ("I See, I See, Mr. Matter") in a special issue devoted to television of the magazine *Eñe* (La Fábrica, 2007).

"Kidney" ("Ronyó") was commissioned for publication in the book *El llibre de la Marató de TV3* (Edicions 62,

2011), which was a fund-raiser for the television marathon devoted to organ and tissue regeneration and transplants.

"The Miracle of the Loaves and the Fishes" ("El miracle dels pans i els peixos") was serialized in shorter format as a summer vacation story, from August 15 to 19, 2016, in the newspaper *El Periódico*, where it was titled "Destí Las Vegas" ("Destination Las Vegas").

"Vertical" is included in the jointly authored anthology *Gira Barcelona* (Comanegra, 2016). This time the conditions of the commission were precisely defined: the story had to be set in Barcelona, between ten and twelve at night, in the month of June, and it had to be written in the third person and the present tense.

"Blinker" ("Intermitent") appears in an anthology titled *Risc* (:Rata_, 2017), by several authors and, more than a commission, it was an invitation, since there were no prior stipulations apart from intrinsic literary risk.

"Patience" ("La paciència") arose from an invitation by the Goethe Institute of Germany to take part in the *Hausbesuch* (Home Visit) project together with eight other writers from around Europe. After spending some days in Hamburg and Nancy, and having dinner in four homes, two in each city to which I'd been invited, I was to write a short story based on the conversations, walks, and experiences of those days. The results of the project were published in ebook form (Frohmann Verlag, 2017) in seven languages: Catalan, Spanish, German, French, Italian, Dutch, and Portuguese.

About the Author

JORDI PUNTÍ was born in 1967 and lives in Barcelona. He is mainly a fiction writer, and a regular contributor to the Spanish and Catalan press. He has published three books of short stories, and the novel *Lost Luggage*, which won numerous prizes, including the Premi Llibreter, the Catalan booksellers prize, and has been translated into more than sixteen languages. He's also the author of *Els castellans* (*The Castilians*), a memoir on the relationship in the 1970s between Catalan kids and the immigrants who arrived from Spain to an industrial town. In 2014 he was a recipient of the fellowship for the Cullman Center for Scholars and Writers, at the New York Public Library, for a fiction project. His most recent book, translated into English, is *Messi. Lessons in Style* (2018), a literary essay collection that explores the genius of one of the best soccer players in the world.